THE
MISSIONARIES

CASTALIA HOUSE

Non-Fiction
MAGA Mindset: Making YOU and America Great Again by Mike Cernovich
SJWs Always Lie by Vox Day
Cuckservative by John Red Eagle and Vox Day
Equality: The Impossible Quest by Martin van Creveld
A History of Strategy by Martin van Creveld
4th Generation Warfare Handbook by William S. Lind and LtCol Gregory
    A. Thiele, USMC
Compost Everything by David the Good
Grow or Die by David the Good

Fiction
Brings the Lightning by Peter Grant
The Missionaries by Owen Stanley

Science Fiction
The End of the World as We Knew It by Nick Cole
CTRL-ALT REVOLT! by Nick Cole
Awake in the Night Land by John C. Wright
Somewhither by John C. Wright
Back From the Dead by Rolf Nelson
Victoria: A Novel of Fourth Generation War by Thomas Hobbes

Military Science Fiction
There Will Be War Volumes I and II ed. Jerry Pournelle
There Will Be War Volumes IX and X ed. Jerry Pournelle (forthcoming)

Fantasy
Iron Chamber of Memory by John C. Wright

Audiobooks
A History of Strategy narrated by Jon Mollison
Cuckservative narrated by Thomas Landon
Four Generations of Modern War narrated by William S. Lind
Grow or Die narrated by David the Good
Extreme Composting narrated by David the Good
A Magic Broken narrated by Nick Afka Thomas

THE
MISSIONARIES

OWEN STANLEY

The Missionaries

Owen Stanley

Published by Castalia House
Kouvola, Finland
www.castaliahouse.com

Editor: Vox Day

Contents

Chapter I

THE PIPER AZTEC flew out of the clouds, and the jagged green mass of Elephant Island appeared beneath the nose, dead ahead. Long ages since, huge volcanic forces had thrust its mountains from the sea bed, their crests streaming lava and plumes of sulphurous smoke in the South Pacific Trades. Then the gentler but no less determined forces of wind and rain had moulded it, bringing and nurturing the seeds that clothed it in luxuriant forests, and the rivers to cut deep valleys through the ranges, washing down the silt of millennia to fill the wide swamps at the eastern end.

And now, to this indolent and undemanding home of primitive men was coming a force of change mightier than lava and earthquake, fire and landslide. Dr. Sydney Prout, Ph.D London, and sometime Lecturer in Sociology at Manchester, was the Head of the United Nations Mission to Elephant Island. Incredibly emaciated, his gaunt frame was crowned with a bony head whose chief features were a covering of ginger bristles on the scalp and two piercing grey eyes.

"There she is," said Ross McLennan, the pilot, "Elephant Island."

"But there aren't any elephants in the Pacific. What a ridiculous name."

"There was one once. Belonged to Blackbird McGarvey, old-time skipper. Fell for a chief's daughter, but her old man sized up his schooner, and reckoned a man with a canoe that big could cough up with one hell of a big pig for his daughter. Blackbird tried every dodge he could think of to get the girl, but it was no go. The chief had it stuck in his head that the white man had everything bigger than the brown man, and wanted his cut. Well, Blackbird was stumped for a time, till one day he was in Sydney when the circus was in town. They had a sick young elephant and wanted to unload it on some sucker, which was Blackbird. He paid a fortune for it, clapped it in the hold, brought it out here, put on his top hat and fancy waistcoat, and let it out on the beach to claim his beloved. The locals took one look and shit 'emselves. Took off into the bush and didn't come out for a month. He never got the girl, neither—she'd pissed off with her old man. And Blackbird got clobbered by a typhoon and his ship went down with all hands. Unlucky sort of bloke really."

"What happened to the elephant?"

"Dunno. I s'pose the locals kai-kaied it when they'd worked up enough guts for the job. These coastal bastards look good enough on a picture postcard, but one whiff of a mountain man and they're up the palm trees so fast you'd think there was red-hot pokers up their bums."

Prout frowned; the crudely contemptuous racialism of the pilot came as a shock, even though he had read about such attitudes in the *Journal of Race Relations*. He adroitly diverted the conversation into more strictly sociological channels.

"These mountain people, are they as ferocious as their reputations?"

"Oh, yeah, they're a rough mob all right. They're called Moroks. But Roj has 'em pretty well tamed. Gets on well with 'em too."

"Roj?"

"He's the RM—Resident Magistrate. Roger Fletcher's his name. They call him "Roaring Roger" around here. Good bloke when you get to know 'im. Very practical."

Prout pursed his lips. "Practical." Anyone whom the likes of McLennan called "practical" almost certainly despised sociology and was prone to ignoring proper administrative procedure. "Well, from what we've heard in New York he doesn't seem to have been very successful. That's why we're taking over."

"Yeah. I heard you blokes were giving Australia the push. You don't reckon we're up to the job, is that it?"

"Oh, not at all. But unfortunately Australia has allowed an un-qualified, and really, a very reactionary man, to have his own way with the island for so long that no social or economic progress has been made at all. At this stage in the process of decolonisation, Australia feels it would be less embarrassing for her if the United Nations assumed the responsibility for preparing the indigenous people for independence. That's why I'm here."

Ross digested this information and being, like most professional pilots, a resigned and imperturbable man, he said nothing. He merely cut back the power and put the aircraft into a shallow descent, to take them over the coastline at an altitude of 5,000 feet.

"The airstrip's up in the mountains, around 3,000 feet up. Climate's bloody terrible on the coast—all mozzies and swamp. The Yanks were here during the war and put the strip in up at Ungabunga. But the RM's always lived there. By the way, we're just flying over Byron Bay now."

"Don't tell me that Lord Byron came here looking for a wife too."

The pilot flashed him an amused grin. "No, nothin' like that. Just the first RM, Carstairs, a bloody loony. They all seem to end up here. This one had a thing about the great poets. Have a look at the chart. Ruddy poets' names all over."

As they passed over the beaches below, Ross brought the nose of the plane up and boosted the power to check their descent, then levelled out. The great peaks of Shakespeare and Milton rose ahead of them, with Wordsworth a little to the rear. Even at eleven in the morning clouds were drifting near the summits.

They flew on in silence, and Prout surveyed his new responsibilities as they passed below. Near the coast were a few scattered villages among the mangrove and sago swamps that were cut into fragments of lagoon by the greasy waters of the Ungabunga River as it moved slowly towards the open sea, dully reflecting the sun. Up ahead were the ranges, monotonously green, upon whose flanks was not the smallest indication of human habitation or activity.

As they reached the point where the Ungabunga debouched from its mountain prison, Ross banked the plane and they turned into a valley which had somehow escaped the literary ravages of the first Resident Magistrate. The spurs began to rise beneath them, and soon Prout could see tiny settlements of leaf-thatched huts and scattered gardens in the forest, and along the backs of ridges he saw spidery tracks of red clay that stood out clearly against the green. In the bottom of the valley foamed the waters of the Ungabunga.

The walls of the valley were rising steadily around them, and after a few minutes Ross banked to the left and turned into a tributary gorge; soon he pointed to a spur below them, on Prout's side, and shouted "Ungabunga!"

Two thousand feet below them the strip could be plainly seen, overshadowed at one end and along one side by the almost vertical wall of the mountainside, with a precipice dropping sheer into the river at the other end, by the wind sock. At the top of the strip under the mountain was a stockaded fort with various buildings inside, while more structures lined the side of the strip along the mountain wall.

But even at this height it was obvious that their arrival was unexpected, to say the least. The strip was occupied by what appeared to be two ranks of people facing each other, with another group at the fortress end. Ross let down some flap and put the plane into a left-hand circuit, which obscured Prout's view, but as they circled lower they saw the two ranks charge together and begin hacking at each other with barbaric vigour. By the time Ross had brought the plane down to one thousand feet above the strip, they could see that the parties to the dispute were small, furious, dark-skinned men clad in feathers, busily engaged in battering the daylights out of each other with wooden clubs.

"It seems that I've arrived only just in time," Prout commented thoughtfully.

Chapter II

AT DAWN, while Prout was still abed in Rabaul, the villagers of Niovoro and Lavalava had already begun the fifteen-mile hike down the track from their mountain refuge to Ungabunga. The path swung down among the spurs and creeks, steadily descending, an even red ribbon of law and order against the jungle above and below it, blasted and hacked under government orders twenty years before, but still wide enough to allow a horse or a motor-bike to pass, and, of course, the silent feet of the Moroks.

Although it was officially the dry season, there had been heavy rain in the night and the grass beside the track sparkled with unfallen drops that drenched the legs of the men as they thrust their way past. The night air still lay cold in the valleys, and breath came in clouds. They were small men, mountain men, the corded muscles of their legs knotted and stressed by years of merciless exertion on mountainside and track. Their heads were brilliant with the plumage of cockatoo and bird of paradise, and their faces were painted with vivid ochres and stained with the juices of wild berries, but their eyes gleamed coldly beneath heavy and protruding brows. Through their hooked, pendulous noses were thrust the curving tusks of the wild boar, whose points swept up towards those glittering, manic eyes. Around their waists were suspended girdles of human thigh-bones.

The hurrying files of men bristled with bows; bunches of arrows, some tipped with slivers of scrap iron; quivering spears of the black palm wood, serrated and barbed to rip out the bowels of enemies; and clubs: smooth clubs for braining pigs, knotted and gnarled clubs for settling private scores in a single smashing blow, stone clubs, cut into discs for taking a man's head off at the neck, or into the shape of pineapples, to splinter limb bones; and many carried bamboo beheading knives, hardened in the fire, and blackened by use.

Some weapons were new and untried, but others were old companions in many a bloody skirmish and rout, and had names, like trusty dogs. "Skull-Cracker," "Old Blinder," "Beg for Mercy," and "Bloody Ruin," these were all clubs or spears whose fame had been shouted at a hundred dances or more.

Little groups of women, each wearing several string-bags of sweet-potatoes and other vegetables on her back that were suspended from her forehead, moved with the men. They were dowdy creatures, as dour as their menfolk, but without the manic gleam that lighted their husbands' countenances. The breasts of the more mature were flat and sagging, flapping against their chests as they bent forward into their loads.

As the file of men and women drew near the station, groups of them began to congregate by the streams that ran across the track, washing the mud from their legs and, in the case of the men, attending to each other's make-up—a finger-full of red ochre for an eyebrow, the juice of the *mirima* berry to give lustre to a forehead, a streak of white clay for a nose.

The sun, though now well risen, had not yet driven off the mists from all the ridges; at intervals came the drawn-out cries of men calling to one another from spur to spur along the cliff-side track. Those strange, echoing cries, wailing through the mists and gorges, seemed to have little that was human in them.

At Ungabunga, Roger Fletcher, the Resident Magistrate of Her Britannic Majesty's Possession of Elephant Island, Warden of the Goldfields, Justice of the Peace, Receiver of Wrecks, Comptroller of Excises, Coroner, and High Bailiff, leaned over the verandah of his fort and spat on a lizard. He had come to the end of his cigarette, and the rusty-brown, scuttling creature sunning itself beside the steps was the most satisfying target he could find for a fat gob of nicotine-flavored spit. Then he dug into his pocket for a lighter and lit another.

He was a man in his late thirties, of nearly six foot, and broad, with black hair and beard in which beads of sweat trickled and glistened. His eyes were blue. His hands were thrust into his khaki riding breeches, the fly of which was broken and permanently exposed. The breeches ended in gaitered brown boots, while the upper part of his body was clad in a khaki shirt, topped off by an Army-surplus bush hat. The cigarette, of native tobacco rolled in newspaper, hung from his lips, emitting a smell which most people encounter only at burning rubbish dumps, the unmistakable aroma of smouldering mattresses and blackened tins. But he liked it. Especially on the first Monday in the month, which was land dispute day at Ungabunga.

"Who's on the card today, Olly?" he shouted, half turning his head towards the door of the office which led off the verandah. His voice was harsh and grating.

In the gloom of the office a vast white shape, "like a slug in a bell tent," as Fletcher described it, slowly stirred. Oelrichs, Assistant Resident Magistrate, was shifting his twenty-three stone bulk in its strengthened *tsiga* wood chair, the better to consult the schedule of land disputes and see which villages were settling their differences that day.

"Niovoro and Lavalava seem to be the only ones listed," he called; "Sapo and Ganipa scratched on account of the dysentery."

He resumed his work on the compilation of some fictitious venereal disease returns for the police, a task which on this occasion called for unusual finesse. Unlike Fletcher, Oelrichs had a marked aversion to physical exercise, dressed entirely in white silk, and had seldom walked a step in the last ten years, preferring the amenities of his sedan chair and its four groaning bearers, recruited from the gaol. There were no shortage of them; to volunteer as bearer for the Assistant Resident Magistrate automatically earned the local law-breakers a half-remission of sentence.

When in the office, Oelrichs devoted his not inconsiderable intellect to compiling fraudulent returns on every item of station equipment from asbestos blankets to zinc ointment, and fictitious reports on social, political, economic, educational, moral, agricultural, sanitary, religious, and meteorological progress to a mercifully distant Department in Canberra. When not in the office, he devoted the same single-minded attention to eating, either as the guest of Madame Negretti at the Cosmopolitan Hotel, Ungabunga's only pub, or in his own exquisite quarters, where his furnishings were sumptuous, his cellar catholic, and his hospitality proverbial.

The Government office was a highly defensible structure of mud and timber, loop-holed for rifle fire in all directions, and surrounded by a high stockade and a ditch. The only entrance, facing the airstrip, was guarded by a timber gatehouse, and closed at night. Within the stockade were storehouses, armoury, and orderly room and guard room, with a well. Above all flew the Australian flag. Below the small hill on which it stood, and to the left, were the gaol, barracks for the police, the pub, a trade-store, a few houses for the European residents, and a clutter of native hovels.

The airstrip was now rapidly filling with natives from Lavalava and Niovoro, and hundreds of spectators from other villages. The police, resplendent in spiked helmets, were waving cavalry sabres and disarming the combatants as they entered the station at the far end of the airstrip, and piling their weapons in heaps. The weapons were kept under police guard, although the natives received cudgels as replacements and were allowed to keep their shields. The men of Lavalava and Niovoro, driven by the curses of the police, were separated into their respective groups, facing each other across the strip, from which positions they began bombarding each other with obscene repartee, slapping their bare buttocks in derision. Their women, from the spectators' area, urged them on to atrocious acts. Four mounted constables on horses patrolled the space between the contending parties to prevent any unsporting attempt to begin the proceedings before the arrival of the umpire.

On the verandah of the office Fletcher had been joined by Oelrichs, but they were almost instantly interrupted by the thudding of nailed boots up the steps and along the verandah. The sergeant-major was coming to report all correct for the first event of the day, and to request the presence of the Resident Magistrate. Eighteen stone and six feet four inches of Binandere warrior crashed to attention before the Resident Magistrate, hand quivering at the salute, spike of helmet glinting, pace-stick rigid under arm, little piggy eyes glaring into middle distance, the dust settling around the huge black boots at an angle of 45 degrees and casting a faint haze over the winking gloss of the toe caps. Once, he had been a tribesman from New Guinea, but now he was of the tribe of sergeant-majors, found wherever a flagstaff flies the Union Jack, who dream not of crocodiles and sorcery, but of metal polish and fire buckets, defaulters' parades, and idle kit.

"All he come, sah. All kanaka on parade."

"Very good. Carry on, Sergeant-Major." Fletcher returned the salute; the sergeant-major about-turned, and signalled to the garrison buglers, who began their flourishes as the RM made his way behind the sergeant-major's stately tread to the rostrum outside the stockade. Once he was seated under a brilliant canopy fashioned from a cargo of gaudy second-hand underwear intended for a missionary congregation in the Solomons, but piously diverted by Oelrichs as being dangerous to their faith and morals, the buglers fell silent, and the proper business of the day began.

The two chiefs of Lavalava and Niovoro, Abuk and Deng, approached the dais and attempted to salute. The sergeant-major, standing rigidly at attention by the steps, shuddered, and wished fervently to have them in his drill squad for a whole, hot, afternoon.

"O Tikame," said Abuk in the Morok language, which Fletcher spoke fluently, "O Tikame, thou well knowest these dung piles of Niovoro, how their women stink so foul that only the wild boars of the forest can abide to mount them, how the cods of their young men hang tiny and shrivelled like the smallest finger of an aged crone, how they feed their guests on dogs' turds, now, and now"—his voice rose to a shriek of anguished rage—"these half-men, these bush pigs, dare to claim the sacred land of our fathers, the land called Arafura, bounded by the pandanus palms and by the Lava river, of me and my brothers. Thou knowest well, O mighty Tikame, that words of truth fall as often from the lips of men like these as riches from the arses of our pigs. Give us leave, then, to smite this offal, utterly to destroy them, and drive them from thy sight, that even their pigs shall flee them for shame."

"What sayest thou, O Deng?" Fletcher looked to the chief of the Niovoro.

Deng, half of whose face had been smashed in by a club when he was young, and who had been gazing at Abuk in silent contempt during his frenzied harangue, produced a handful of feathers from behind his back and replied.

"O Tikame, we men of Niovoro heed not these bird songs of the Lavalava. For the Lavalava are like unto these feathers that when the wind bloweth upon them, are scattered over the earth, and are seen no more." He blew the feathers away, and they were taken up by the wind. "That is all my speech. Let us to arms, O Tikame."

"So be it," said Fletcher, waving them back to their places to await his signal. The two chiefs departed to the ranks of their men, and the RM welcomed a number of Europeans onto the dais, including Oelrichs, who had just arrived in his creaking palanquin.

Tikame was the mightiest of the Morok folk-heroes, half man, half spirit, who had roamed their mountains in the dawn of antiquity, a great hunter, law-giver, and breaker of heads. The Moroks were convinced that Fletcher was a reincarnation of this prepotent Being, an illusion that he did nothing to dispel. But native philosophers had been much exercised to find a place in their scheme of things for Oelrichs. Clearly, he was the inseparable companion of Tikame; he was not his wife, equally clearly; and he seemed to spend his life in eating. Garang, the greatest philosopher of the Moroks, had spent many fruitless hours alone on his rock, high above the Lamaipa River, attempting to precisely reconcile these curious features of the relationship between Tikame and his oversized companion.

One afternoon—it was the dry season, when men scurried up and down the tracks with new timbers for garden fences, and women sang to their babies as they gathered up the dried underbrush for burning, and the great valleys were full of the hazy smoke from grass fires—the truth dawned upon Garang. Of course: the legends told that Tikame did have a male companion, his inseparable comforter, vast in bulk and fathomlessly cunning. It had been his great pig, Oburabu. The true identity of Oelrichs was discovered at last!

"Amazing," thought Garang, as he made his way back to the

men's house in his village to spread the news of this revelation. "Amazing how one can penetrate the red men's secrets, if one only thinks clearly and patiently. They're almost human."

Fletcher and Oelrichs were joined on the dais by the other Europeans of the station—"Smith," the doctor; Madame Negretti, proprietress of the Cosmopolitan Hotel; Ned Oakley, a gold miner down for the week-end from his camp at Armpit Creek; and Erny English, storekeeper and airline agent.

"Smith" was really Wladislaw Prsloczlawski, a cheerful Pole who had been rechristened Smith on his arrival by Fletcher, who refused "to have a bloody disgustin' set o' noises like that on me clean station register." Although Smith was a doctor, his real interests lay with the dead, not the living, since the focus of his life was pathology. Every morning, his eyes roamed over the patients in his dispensary, as they lolled against the grime-encrusted, shiny plaster walls, probing each hopefully in turn for some sign of mortal decay, some festering lesion in a vital organ that would bring them swiftly to his mortuary slab, and perhaps to the ultimate distinction of the pickling jar, most of which came from Madame Negretti's kitchen when she could find no fruit suitable for bottling. His autopsies, at which sherry was served, were one of the few bright spots on the Ungabunga social calendar.

Madame Negretti was an Italian lady, of ample proportions, the widow of a sea captain, with beady eyes but a jolly sense of humour. Her hobbies were cooking, at which she was superb, and knitting, at which she was exceedingly bad. In moments of agitation, her cardigans and bed-jackets were apt to disintegrate into a mess of tangled cordage and broken spars, resembling the rigging of one of Nelson's ships of the line after a prolonged fleet action.

Ned Oakley was a small, intensely respectable gold-miner, who wore spectacles and came into Ungabunga once a month on land dispute day to pick up his grub from the store, his copies of *The Tablet* and *The Chess World*, and a case of rum, and to watch the conflicts being resolved, for he prided himself on having a connoisseur's eye for a good scrap.

Erny English came from God knows where. No one knew much about his past, since he was always drunk by ten in the morning, and his steady consumption of rum made conversation between then and bedtime rather laborious.

As soon as the official party was comfortably seated, Fletcher rose and drew his revolver. The police on the strip observed his action, and galloped furiously to safety as he raised the weapon and fired a single shot. Its reverberations were drowned by a mighty yell as the two ranks of frenzied mountain men, their gaping mouths dripping red with betel juice and lifted to heaven as they howled aimlessly, rushed forward to lock themselves in combat.

Cudgels rose and fell, and feather headdresses flew like chaff on the threshing floor. Scalps split, and blood splattered over arms and shoulders and mingled with the ochres and clays on the faces of the warriors. But most of the blows were taken on the shields, and sounded like heavy rain on a palm-leaf roof. At first the men of Lavalava, urged on by the wild shouts of Abuk, pressed the warriors of Niovoro back under the furious impulse of their charge. The ranks swayed this way and that, each side struggling for mastery, but suddenly, under the cool leadership of Deng, the men of Niovoro changed their tactics. Deng and his picked warriors at the centre began delivering devastating body thrusts at the vitals of their enemies, many of whom collapsed writhing and clutching themselves. The Lavalava centre weakened and in a trice was broken by the Niovoro vanguard. Abuk went down to a particularly vicious thrust from Ajiek, brother to the wife of Deng, and the Lavalava, now split in two, turned aside from the furious assault. The Niovoro cudgels fell

instead on kidneys and elbows, and thwacked across muscular buttocks, as the Lavalava broke and ran before the final colossal charge,
flinging away cudgels and shields as they sprinted for safety to the
drainage ditch at the side of the strip. The Niovoro, in the heat of the
charge, would have followed up their advantage and well rubbed-in
their victory with iron fence-posts, rocks, and broken bottles, but
the police, anticipating them, fired a volley over the heads of the
winners with their shotguns, bringing the Niovoro to a halt, dust
rising in clouds around them, now cheerful and exultantly throwing
their cudgels in derision after their scattering foes.

It was only then, as the shouting died, that everyone became
aware of the plane circling low overhead.

Chapter III

Ross TURNED the plane on to final approach, and they glided in across the gorge of the Ungabunga, a thousand feet below. Prout froze as the plane dropped suddenly, and it seemed that they would undershoot and crash into the cliff below the end of the strip, but Ross maintained height, and aimed for a point well beyond the threshold. A gust of cross-wind swung the aircraft for a second, but he dipped his wing and held a straight course with rudder until his main wheels touched, then taxied up the strip, with a burst of power to take the plane over the last few hundred feet to its parking position opposite the trade-store.

As the propellers tick-tocked to a halt, Prout flung open the door and stepped out on to the wing, looking about him. Much to his surprise, after the miniature Armageddon he had witnessed from the air, everything now seemed peaceful. He felt vaguely that his own presence might already have begun to have a steadying effect. And the greater the chaos at the beginning of his administration, the greater would be his credit for restoring order.

His speculations were rudely disturbed by the arrival of Erny, who was by now in the cheerful stage of his alcoholic trajectory, and had come to carry out his duties as airline agent. Seeing a lonely figure poised hesitantly upon the wing, Erny's first thought was to assist the obviously nervous passenger to alight. Staggering forward, he clumsily embraced Prout's ankles:

"Yer just put yer foot there, mate."

The next second, Prout found himself overbalanced. Erny crumpled beneath the unexpected weight, and fell flat on his back as gravity drove one of Prout's bony knees into a sensitive part of the drunkard's anatomy. In response, Erny vomited, noisily and copiously, over Prout's legs. As Prout scrambled to his feet, green and trembling, his brow dewed with sweat, Fletcher and Smith came up.

"Jeez, I'm sorry, mate," groaned Erny. "Didn't mean to hurl over yer strides like that. Just tryin' to help." Clutching himself with one hand, he knelt up and tried to wipe his breakfast from Prout's grey flannels with the other. Prout looked down, horror-stricken.

"Yer a bloody good chunderer, Erny," broke in Fletcher, "But you'd better leave the laundry business to Angelina." He held out his hand to Prout, who took it limply.

"I'm Roger Fletcher, Resident Magistrate. And this is Smithy, the Doc."

"I'm Sydney Prout, United Nations Special Commissioner."

"G'day. We've been expectin' yer. Y'd better come over to the pub. There's a shower there. One of the boys'll fetch yer gear. Look after Ern, Smithy." They began to walk over to the pub.

"Didja have a good trip?"

"Very smooth, thank you."

"Yeh, good. Well, we'll have plenty of time to talk later on today, after dinner."

They had reached the hotel, built of red corrugated iron, with a white verandah of fantastic woodwork around the upper floor, and Fletcher led the way inside. Prout, unhappily aware of the mephitic vapours which enveloped him, was not anxious to linger in company, and went off at once with the "boy" to have his shower and change.

As soon as he had gone, Fletcher steered Ross, who had come in a moment later, over to the bar.

"Well, Ross, that's a weird cargo you brought us. What did yer make of it?"

"Ah, typical bloody do-gooder. Reckons he and the orlies'll be pissin' in each other's pockets in half no time, yer could see that."

"They may, too."

"How d'ya mean?"

"Well, we knew this joker was comin', so we told the locals an old mate of ours is bringin' 'em all kinds of goodies from the sky. I'll take 'im on a walkabout."

"Ya' oughta drop 'im dahn a shit 'ouse, Roj."

"That's Plan B. Plan A is that after a coupl'a months of that Morok sense of humour he goes stark ravin' troppo and gets shipped out in a box with 'oles in it."

"I reckon the first bloke who'll get shipped out is you, Roj."

"The hell I will. Who's gonna interpret for 'im? Who knows the people? He's gotta keep me on whether he likes it or not. Same goes for Olly. You stayin' over till tomorra?"

"Yeh."

"Well don't forget tonight's piss-up night. I'll see yer down 'ere. Get Angelina to keep the prick busy till after dinner. I'll be up at Olly's." And he strode quickly out of the bar and set his course for Oelrichs' residence.

Up in his room, as he tugged off his soiled clothes, Prout brooded on his humiliating entry to Ungabunga, his memory riveted on those hideous moments on the grass, that ruffian heaving and retching, the stench, and the fetid slime gluing his trousers to his legs—faugh! He was a joke, a figure of ridicule, probably at this moment the butt of Australian crudities in the bar downstairs.

But as he relaxed under the soothing waters of the shower he reflected that they had little enough to laugh about, when their own headquarters had just been turned into a battleground. He dried himself carefully, feeling thoroughly cleansed. Yes, absolute chaos—Fletcher had obviously lost his grip completely. The reports had seriously underestimated the social disintegration on the island. Restored, he pulled on a clean pair of flannels and slipped his stockinged feet into some open leather sandals, sank into an easy chair and unlocked his briefcase to prepare for his first official meeting with his new subordinates.

Moia, Madame Negretti's chef from a neighbouring island, was in the kitchen, expertly preparing Quiche Lorraine for lunch and whistling as he sliced the bacon. This was one of his favorite dishes, declared by the epicures of Ungabunga to be surpassed only by his Suprême de Volaille à la Maréchal. But, as the best piano tuners are said to lose their ear if they play the instrument to which their lives are devoted, so Moia never tasted the dishes he so dexterously prepared—the smell and texture were enough. His personal menu was drawn from the simpler repertoire of his tribe: at that very moment a plump, juicy rat lay in the colander ready to be boiled for his lunch. He left the table and went to the larder for some eggs, but as he was putting them in the bowl he heard a crash in the kitchen behind him.

Running back he saw Malvolio, Madame Negretti's cat, leap from the table with his dinner in its jaws. In an instant the veneer of the cook was shed, and he became as his fathers before him, hunters of the wild boar with bow and spear; seizing a cleaver he hurled it at Malvolio, crouching and growling behind the door, and nearly severed the brute's head. Bloody pusscat, he'd had it coming to him all right. Not the first time he'd nicked his dinner. But Missus would be angry. She loved it like his own women loved their baby pigs. Maybe she would call the sergeant and have him put in the calaboose. The vision of hunters in the primeval forest faded, and that of the chef resumed its place. What would he do with the body, its fur now matted with the blood that spread thickly over the concrete floor? Suddenly, he remembered that it was curry night at the Cosmopolitan. He grinned as an idea occurred to him, and in his culinary imagination, as he carried the corpse to the larder, Malvolio was already jointed and simmering in a rich broth.

After an excellent lunch, Prout received word that he would be welcome at the Office to discuss his plans with the Resident Magistrate. The policeman who delivered the invitation conducted him the few hundred yards, and showed him up the steps and into the Office. Facing him was the heaving bulk of Oelrichs, seated at the centre of the table, while Fletcher sat at one end, tilting his chair back against an arms-rack behind him, filled with Lee-Enfields complete with bayonets in black scabbards and green canvas frogs. The inevitable newspaper cigarette hung from his lips. Since it was eight inches long—about half a page from the *Sydney Herald*—he was obviously expecting an intellectually arduous afternoon.

"I don't think you've met Mr Oelrichs. Me right 'and man. Dr Prout, the Special Commissioner."

"How do you do," said Oelrics.

"Pleased to meet you."

"Well, Dr Prout, we've been expecting you. Like to put us in the picture?" said Fletcher.

"I certainly would. I may as well come straight to the point and speak frankly. From all the reports I have studied, it's quite clear that your policies have resulted in social stagnation for the people—no schools, no democratic institutions, no improvement in the standard of living—"

"Yeah, but—"

"Please let me finish. I'm quite prepared to agree that Canberra must bear a great deal of this responsibility, in view of its lax supervision, and I suppose since you obviously have no faith in the ability of these people to operate civilized institutions, your policies are consistent with your beliefs. But one might have expected that, as a practical man, you would at least have been able to maintain law and order. Yet this morning I was unable to land here, at your own headquarters, because the aerodrome was a seething mass of... of... well, what exactly *is* your explanation of the incredible violence which I saw?"

"Just a land dispute being heard by the Court. It's the way we settle things here."

"What *do* you mean?"

"Well, y'see, we know bugger-all about these jokers. Their minds don't work the same as ours. After a few years, y'think y're gettin' to know 'em, and then one morning y'wake up and find y've had it all arse about face from the word go."

"Very likely, I should think."

"Yeah, well, as I was sayin', it's a bloody waste of time tryin' to apply our laws and customs to these blokes. Yer get a coupl'a tribes, next-door neighbours most often. The men are always sneakin' off inter the bush for a naughty with the other blokes' wives, or nickin' each others' pigs, or fellin' each others' trees, out'a spite. It goes on like this for a while, and the bad blood starts boilin' up. So the chiefs get the sorcerers on the job. They get their bags o' tricks out and a few kids die of the screamin' abdabs, and an old granny or two goes potty, and some other bugger dies of the tremblin' toms, and before yer could say "knife," in the old days they'd got the axes out and were hackin' each other up like firewood. Right, says I, I don't want to know the rights and wrongs of it—and with these bastards they're *all* bloody wrong, anyhow—any fightin' and yer get clobbered."

"What do you mean by clobbered?"

"Oh, burnin' villages, shootin' a few pigs, floggin' the hard cases with wet cane, just to let 'em know I'm around, and got my eye on 'em."

"I see. But what's all this got to do with land disputes?"

"Well, it's the same principle, in't it? What the hell can we do when a coupl'a chiefs come to us, and one of 'em says that some piece of land was inherited from his father's mother's brother's wife, who used to live with his granny when her old man died, and the other chief says that she was never married in the first place, but just shacked up with him, and the land was never hers anyway, because she'd accepted two pigs when she was younger not to make a claim on it? So we do the simple thing and bring 'em all down here to fight it out, under police supervision, take their weapons off 'em and give 'em cudgels, and may the best side win. No one gets killed—usually, anyway; the women and kids get an outin', and bring us down some spuds and veggies, Smithy gets some patients, and Erny sells some booze, if he hasn't drunk it all himself, that is. And the kanakas are happy because they've let off some steam, and the side that loses can always have another bash at gettin' the land back any time they like. This one today, Niovoro and Lavalava, that's the second time in eighteen months, in't it, Olly?"

"Yes, about that."

"Anyhow, after the fight they all bugger off home, their nasty little minds schemin' and plottin' the return match, and what obscene names they can call the other blokes. So there's no problem of law and order here."

"I see. Perhaps not. But your whole attitude, all your policies, violate every article in the Declaration of Human Rights."

"If yer could convince me the Moroks *were* human, yer might 'ave a point. Ha! Ha! Ha!"

"Good God! I didn't come here to listen to this racist filth. All I've heard from you this afternoon is the most disgusting, reactionary, and uninformed nonsense. Their minds work differently from ours, indeed! It's long been established science that there are no differences between races in people's minds; the only variations are due to environmental factors and they are as slight as they are superficial. My mission here is to change that environment, by raising their standard of living, and giving them democratic institutions and social justice, and independence from colonial rule. The disgusting brawling which you encourage is merely a symptom of environmental stress and frustration at their lack of opportunity to realise those capacities which they share with the whole of humanity. You have encouraged every man to raise his hand against his neighbour, actually to glory in it, for God's sake, instead of encouraging mutual trust and community harmony. Because they are culturally disadvantaged, due to circumstances beyond their control, you sneer at them—why, you probably kick them!"

"Hell, no. That's what I keep the police for—"

"My God!"

"Well, I tell a lie. I do kick me wives, sometimes, to keep 'em happy."

"Your *wives?*"

"Yeah, sort of. Not legal or anythin', but the orlies think I'm one of their old gods come back to earth, so they don't press the finer points of law. When I'm on patrol and I find a decent looking mary, with a chief for her father, I give 'im a few quid and bring 'er down 'ere for a while. If she gets up the duff she shoots through to her old man again. She does well out of it while she's here, the chiefs want to keep in with me, I can twist the chiefs' arms, and that way we keep in touch with what's goin' on—"

This catalogue of exploitation was too much for Prout. His chair upset with a crash, as he leapt up and strode out through the open door of the verandah, where he paced up and down in silence for some time.

"Poor Prout. You're being a little bit too brutal. We'll have him doing something silly in a minute, like saying he's going to do without us, come what may."

"Yeah, it may come to that, but he's got to find out sometime, so may be it's better to give it 'im in one good dose at the beginnin', give 'im time to digest it."

"I hope you're right."

After a while Prout returned, his face composed, and, picking up his chair, he resumed his seat and took a deep breath before addressing the RM again.

"The pilot told me you were a practical man, Mr Fletcher. I begin to see what he meant. But don't you think it rather demeans your rank by turning your residence into a brothel?"

"It's a funny kind of a brothel, with only one customer and all free. If yer really want to see a whorehouse there's one on the station for the police, just behind Erny's store."

"Really. Most interesting. Tell me about it."

"I'll take yer down and introduce yer, if yer like. As yer may have guessed, the police are not what yer would call "intellectually inclined," so they get bored when they've been back on the station for a few days. Before we set up the puss-puss shop, they'd slope off and start rogerin' the local maries, 'ave a few punch-ups with the menfolk who found them on the job, and come back with gallopin' knob-rot inter the bargain—clap's endemic round here. So we roped in a few maries, fixed a standard tariff—not many items, very unimaginative lot—and have Smithy inspect 'em regular. So everyone's happy. Luckily we've had no bloody missionaries to kick up a fuss for years."

"Were there any? I've never heard of a South Sea island without missionaries of some sort."

"Oh yeah. Some stupid flamin' Yanks. What the hell were they called, Olly?"

"The Cast Your Bread Upon the Waters Mission, if I remember rightly."

"That's it. Bloody loonies, the lot of 'em. Led by a bloke called Frankfurter. Vegetarians. Tried to get the people to kill all their pigs as unclean and live on coconut juice."

"Yes," said Oelrichs, "They had a theory that meat inflamed the passions, and that solid food of any kind caused an awareness of bodily functions that was eminently displeasing to God. Since coconuts don't grow up here they had rather a thin time of it, I recall."

"Did they all starve to death?" asked Prout.

"Probably would've done, except I got 'em first. Best charge I ever laid. Always remember it. 'That you, Herbert Martin Frankfurter, of Ungabunga, did with force of arms most grievously disturb the Peace of our Sovereign Lady the Queen, her Crown and Dignity, in that you, the said Herbert Martin Frankfurter, did feloniously seize five pork chops, a steak and kidney pie, and a German sausage, the property of Ernest English, of Ungabunga.' They'd all been living on tinned carrot juice for three months, so no wonder they were flamin' troppo. Fit to be tied, the lot of 'em. Came down from the mission, bright yeller and rollin' their eyes, lookin' like three mad Chinamen—Vitamin B poisoning, Smithy said. Erny'd just got his freezer goods from Rabaul, and they went for 'im like mad dogs. Poor bastard got out the back door with his shirt half off his back. Well, anyhow, the sergeant-major and I quieted 'em down, and shipped 'em out. Been peaceful ever since."

"Yes, well, I'm quite relieved. There's enough superstition in the world without missionaries adding to it. What we need here are facts and clear thinking, and the United Nations is here to provide them. It's obvious that as regards policy, there is no communication at all between us. But I've decided that while I totally disapprove of your methods and attitudes, as a practical necessity I shall have to ask if you are prepared to remain on a temporary basis for the time being—under my immediate supervision, of course. I'm not so naive as to imagine that I can do my job, even with my staff, if I have no one who knows the people and can liase with them. Are you both prepared to stay under those conditions?"

"We imagined you would be bringing your own experts, Dr. Prout, and would have no need of us, so we hadn't expected to stay on," Oelrichs said.

"Oh, of course, I'll be bringing a large staff of experts, but local knowledge is indispensable in a case like this. I think we all understand one another. I'm very disturbed by what I've found here, obviously, and I'll probably be still more disturbed as I learn more, but much of the blame lies with Canberra for their laxity. As I say, you are both free to stay on, at your present salaries, under my orders, for the next year. By that time, if all goes well, independence will be approaching, and we should be able to go our separate ways."

"I think Mr. Oelrichs and I had better have a word in private, before we give you a decision."

"That's quite all right. I'll step outside for a few minutes." He nodded, and returned to the verandah.

"Well, dear boy, that all went very nicely," said Oelrichs, "We'd better give him a few minutes outside, to make him think we're having trouble making up our minds, though."

"Yeah, we'll call him back when I've rolled me cigarette and give

him the good news. You didn't say much. What do y'make of 'im,
being a fellow Pom and all that?"

"Well, certainly a fine specimen of the high-minded interferer.
But not a man to be under-rated—no fool within his limits, and
he knows it. So I think we should play on his vanity, let him think
we accept he's won, that the old order has gone for good, and that
we only want to spend the rest of our time here in peace and quiet,
clinging to our rapidly vanishing privileges."

"Yeah, he should swaller that okay. Righto. I'll call him back.
Dr. Prout!"

After a few moments Prout entered and resumed his seat.

"Well, Mr. Oelrichs and I've agreed that times've changed, and
there's no point in whingein' about it. So it'd suit us to stay on and
work for you for a bit."

"Good. Very sensible. I thought you'd see it like that when you'd
thought it over. I'll leave you in charge of routine administration,
though of course all judicial matters will have to be discharged under
my supervision. There is one other thing. I'll being returning to
Rabaul in a few days to organize my staff, but while I'm here I should
like to have a closer look at the people. Try to get an idea of their
problems. So I should like to go on a brief tour of inspection with
you, if that could be arranged?"

"Oh yeah. No trouble. When do yer want ter leave?"

"Would tomorrow be all right?"

"Yep. Three days' patrol suit yer?"

"I think so."

"Can yer ride a horse?"

"No, I can't. I'm afraid I never had the chance to learn horseback
riding."

"What about a motorbike?"

"A motorbike? I really don't approve of that. You see, mechanical devices create more barriers between us and the indigenous people than anything else. In fact, only last year, I published a paper on the racist implications of air-conditioning in the tropics."

"Most interesting, Dr. Prout," said Oelrichs. "Perhaps you are also familiar with a most stimulating paper, by Wilbur Smallpiece, if I remember rightly, on the fascist connotations of table linen in developing countries?"

"No, I'm afraid not, but it sounds very perceptive. Could you let me have the reference?"

"By all means. I'll look it out, although I'm fairly sure that it was in the *American Anthropologist*.

"Well, Dr. Prout," said Fletcher, with some impatience, "it looks as if you'll have to walk it, so you won't see much of the country in three days."

"I realise that. But the more intense quality of the relationship that I shall attain with the people by walking will be ample compensation."

"Oh yeah? Well, you should know. I'll get it laid on for yer."

"Excellent. I won't detain you any more. But I should like to have a look at a few basic records—census data, court records, and so on."

"Certainly," said Oelrichs. "If you'd like to come through to the other office I'll get them out for you."

Prout finally left with a number of volumes and spent the rest of the afternoon in his hotel room studying them carefully. At last, his investigation complete, he lit another cigarette.

"Very curious," he thought. Fletcher's regime had clearly driven the Moroks to violence—indecent assault, riotous behaviour, arson, rape, and malicious wounding figured prominently in the court records. But there was not a single case of wilful murder, or even manslaughter, in the whole ten years covered by the volumes he had just examined. So how could the people have been so successfully restrained from homicide when every other form of violence was so common? It didn't make sense. Unless... was it possible that the records had been deliberately falsified? But why? After some time a revolting possibility occurred that made him begin to see Fletcher in a very different and truly criminal light. And if he were right, he would not rest until he had brought the man to justice.

Chapter IV

DINNER THAT EVENING at the Cosmopolitan was not a success, in spite of the excellent curry. Madame Negretti was not her usual ebullient self, being grieved and anxious over the disappearance of Malvolio.

"Bush-kanakas them bad buggers past all, Missus," Moia had said, in his most unctuous tones. "Them kaikai pusscat, sure thing."

Prout did his best to entertain the company with reminiscences of his university life at Manchester, but those recollections of wit and brilliancy for which Manchester is celebrated were tinged with melancholy in the very act of being retrieved from memory, those days once so tangible, and yet now so far beyond recall. Fletcher and Smith exchanged notes on infestations of body lice with professional relish, and Erny fell down the stairs. But in spite of these diversions, it was with some relief that the party dispersed to bed soon after ten o'clock.

The next morning was brilliant and clear, and Prout stepped out of the hotel door after breakfast with a look of eager anticipation, shouldering his rucksack for the walk up to the fort. Fletcher and Sgt Oala were outside the fort gate making a final check of the patrol boxes, directing the six policemen who stood close by, some leaning on their .303s. After Prout and Fletcher had exchanged greetings, Prout said: "Well, it's after eight, shouldn't we be moving?"

"No carriers yet. I've sent the corporal to raus 'em."

"Carriers? But surely the police will carry anything that is necessary?"

Fletcher was in an unusually ill humour, since he had slept badly and last night's curry had brought on a nasty attack of his piles.

"The police! For Christ's sake, they're fighting men, not coolies! How d'ya expect 'em to keep order and be respected if they're lumbered with cooking pots and bloody bedding?"

Prout was taken aback.

"Well, I wouldn't know about that. But I can't tolerate this kind of exploitation. What my wife would say if she saw me lording it over a gang of native porters I shudder to think!"

Fletcher exploded.

"I couldn't give a bugger what she'd say. If yer won't go by horse, and yer won't go by bike, ye've gotta have carriers. If yer won't have carriers, yer can bloody well stay at 'ome, so make yer mind up, will yer?"

"I have already explained my wishes. Will you please tell the police to carry the boxes, and forget this nonsense about carriers?"

"If yer wanta insult my police, yer tell 'em yerself."

Flushed with rage, Prout turned to the police, who had been watching the growing anger between the two white men with perplexity and embarrassment.

"You men, there will be no carriers today or at any other time. You will carry the boxes yourselves. Hurry up now, we must get moving." He gesticulated, and spoke rapidly in a higher pitch than usual. The police shifted uneasily, and looked at each other and then to Fletcher for guidance. He winked, and grinned at them.

"Yer might as well save yer breath. They don't understand a ruddy word yer sayin'. Do yer want to go on this patrol or don't yer?"

Seeing the blank incomprehension in the eyes of the police, and catching the grin with which Fletcher had reassured them, Prout hesitated, and bit back the flood of humiliated rage that was about to spew over them all. He was beaten, but still had enough self-control not to make a complete fool of himself.

"Very well. I obviously have no choice. But at least I shall carry my own rucksack." He turned away, and looked fixedly across the valley. Fletcher said to the police:

"Master he no savvy talk belong you-me. Him he say you fellow police lose him carrier, so walkabout belong master all buggerup."

The police laughed. Just as Fletcher was about to bellow down to the jail, Cpl Barigi and the eight convicts who were to carry for the patrol could be seen coming at the double. In less than a minute they had caught up to the patrol, and began shouldering the poles which had been passed through the handles of the three big, galvanized, patrol boxes, two men to a pole, while the last two carriers gathered up an assortment of odds and ends—a couple of folding canvas chairs, hurricane lamps, bowls and buckets—and without more ado the police set off up the left-hand track behind the fort with Sgt Oala leading. After wandering for many miles through the mountains, the track returned by a different route to the station, where it completed the circle. As Prout turned to look at the policemen they grinned at him cheerfully, and settled their rifles for the long climb, holding them by their muzzles over their shoulders.

"We go in the middle," said Fletcher. Prout hoisted his rucksack onto his back, and the carriers, with Cpl Barigi and another constable bringing up the rear, followed them out of the station. The patrol wound its way up the track at a brisk pace; Fletcher maintained silence out of anger and contempt for Prout, and Prout, under the growing weight of his rucksack, found that he had little breath left for talk. Every now and then, his boots slipped off water-polished boulders as they crossed a stream-bed, making him stumble, or turned over as he placed a foot on some uneven ground, causing him to stagger sideways with the pain in the callouses of his feet. Specks of diamond-hard grit were thrown up by his boots and lodged in the tops, quickly working their way down to the soles of his feet, which soon felt red-hot with the unaccustomed irritation.

The track at this stage traversed an almost waterless part of Mount Browning, and as the streams ran only in a brief spate after rainstorms, the beds were now bone-dry. The spur faced east, and by ten o'clock the sun was beating hotly down upon the mountainside. Only coarse grass grew here, since all the trees had long since been burnt off by the natives, to make gardens, which had themselves been abandoned many years before.

Prout's saliva began to dry up and turn into a thick, white slime that coated the inside of his mouth. It ran down the back of his throat and formed a froth under his tongue. He began to hawk and spit to try to dislodge it, and his breathing became louder and hoarser. The straps of the rucksack cut into his flesh, and his shoulders ached dully with the effort of sustaining its weight. To keep up appearances, he gasped at Fletcher.

"Those rocks up ahead, a very interesting shape."

"Yeh. That's where we'll have a sipelli."

"A what?"

"A spell, a smoko. Not far."

The rocks, an outcrop of yellow-grey granite, blasted and splintered by dynamite when the track had been put through, marked the crest of the ridge up whose side they were toiling. Beyond the pinnacles the track turned sharply into the next valley. Prout began to estimate the distance still to be covered—perhaps a mile. At three miles an hour that should take twenty minutes. Thank God, he ought to be able to hold on until then. The path turned right,

into another re-entrant, for the umpteenth time; this one was unusually steep-sided, shadowed and echoing, but with no trace of water. They picked their way across the ruckle of boulders at its centre;
Prout stumbled badly, and the breath was jarred from his body as he
gasped and staggered and barely managed to keep his feet. Before he
could recover it, he found the path rising more steeply than ever; his
legs drove down like pistons as he dug in his toes, his breath coming in a series of grunts and wheezes. Under his armpits, dark stains
spread over his shirt, reeking sourly of sweat and reaching more than
half way to his belt, while under the pack his shirt was clinging and
sodden. The gap between the police and himself was widening, as
they drew away with easy strides, while the carriers, seemingly unaware of their swaying burdens, pressed upon him and Fletcher, who
was content to adjust his pace to Prout's.

As they emerged from the re-entrant and rounded the next corner, the rocks appeared again on the horizon, perhaps a little nearer.
The altitude was beginning to take effect, as they were now at more
than five thousand feet. He could feel his pulse beating in his tem-
ples, and his vision periodically grew dim; the roar of the Ungabunga
river, thousands of feet below, advanced and receded like waves on
the sea shore.

The path swung into another re-entrant, and the rocks vanished
from sight again. A sudden gust of scorching wind from the valley
below roared over the path, driving up a cloud of dust and sand.
Prout put his hand over his eyes and caught his foot on a boulder,
stumbling and almost falling again. His sweat poured out in torrents. The second pair of carriers passed them. The stream bed in
the gully was the steepest so far, and the rain of two nights before
had produced a considerable spate that had badly damaged the track,
tearing away a section until only a narrow ledge was left for passage,
and even this was several feet below the level of the path. As Prout,

now staggering, came up to this obstacle, moaning and wheezing, the rest of the carriers slipped past and dropped nimbly into the stream bed with their loads, vaulted up onto the other bank, and disappeared round the next corner.

Gasping, Prout sank to his knees, and gingerly put one foot over the edge of the bank. The path here was scarcely two feet wide, and formed the lip of a great dry waterfall, Oiburi-Naiburi, whose precipitous faces were sounded by the rocks which Prout dislodged, crashing and volleying until they were lost in the vegetation far below. Slowly, facing inwards to the cliff, he edged his way across, his knees shaking, the weight of the rucksack unbalancing him all the more easily due to the agony in his feet. The far side was steeper and needed more concentration and agility than he commanded. He put his left foot blindly on what was no hold at all, grabbed for the rim, and as he raised his other leg the gravel gave way and he fell back with a shriek of terror. Fletcher caught him, and pressed him against the side of the cliff. After giving him a moment to regain his composure, Fletcher put his hand under Prout's foot and heaved him up over the edge. As Fletcher followed him up, their eyes met. Fletcher's gaze was remote and impersonal.

As they rounded the next bend Prout saw that the rocks had come appreciably nearer, and that the track was level and fairly broad. In another half-hour they reached the resting place, and found the police and carriers sitting and smoking in the shade, or lying half asleep. Prout threw off his rucksack and collapsed like a dead man. It was nearly two hours after he had first seen the rocks.

"Water," he begged. "For God's sake, isn't there any water here?"

"No. Another half-hour," said Fletcher. "Anyhow, it'll do yer no good to drink water. Just slop about in yer guts and slow yer down." He went over to a bag and took out some oranges.

"Have one of these." Prout took it silently, and ravenously tore off the skin, cramming the segments into his mouth so that the juice ran all down his chin.

"Thanks. That was *very* good. Would you have another, by any chance?" As Prout ate the second orange, Fletcher rolled himself a short newspaper cigarette, which he puffed luxuriously in between bites of his own orange. From the rocks they could now survey the great valley which opened before them, its higher slopes thickly carpeted in rain forest. Both sides of the valley were broken by spurs which ran down to a river, a tributary of the Ungabunga, and on each of these spurs could be seen native villages, of palm-leaf thatched hovels, bleached almost white by the sun.

But Prout was too dazed to take in any of this. He lay, a broken and disgusting object, in the shade, his belly rising and falling with his stertorous breathing. He did not notice Fletcher's signal to the carriers and police to be on their way, nor see him point to Prout's rucksack and a carrier whisk it off to be stowed with the rest of the impedimenta. Some minutes after they had gone, Prout roused himself and began to take a passably intelligent interest in his surroundings. When he had surveyed the valley, he said:

"How far do we go today?"

"We'll be at the first village by about half two or three. That's Laripa. We'll have kai there, and hear the talk, have a kip and go on in the morning. The carriers'll have the rest house ready by the time we arrive. C'mon, we'd better get movin'." Prout dragged himself to his feet, his wretched, red-hot feet, and looked around for his rucksack.

"Where's my pack, my pack?" he said in a bewildered way.

"The carriers took it on."

"They *what*? How dare they?"

"Just felt sorry for yer. Anyhow, if they hadn't carried yer pack they'd've ended up carryin' yer instead." He forebore to mention that the carriers had taken the pack on his instructions, or that he had told the police before the patrol began to maintain the hottest possible pace to the rocks, with none of the usual breathers on the way.

"But it's extremely valuable—supposing they drop it over a cliff?"

"Valuable my arse. I wish they'd bloody well drop yer over a cliff. Now for Christ's sake get a move on,"and he walked off up the track without another word. Prout followed sullenly; the release from the crushing burden of the pack gave his legs a spring-like bounce that made him feel almost weightless, but if he was now spared the encumbrance of the pack, his spirits were weighed down by guilt instead. For, despite his best intentions, he was now an exploiter of native labour and, however unwillingly, he had become part of the vile colonialist machine. He had, at the outset of his mission, endangered that fragile bond of respect which he needed to build between himself and those entrusted to his care. His self-flagellating reverie was disturbed by two rifle shots and the notes of a bugle up in front.

"Is that your police attacking some poor villagers?"

"No, worse luck. Just the bugler letting Laripa know we're coming, and tellin' 'em to get firewood cut, and water from the creek."

"Why the shooting?"

"To remind orly that we're the bosses."

"Is that all you can think of—oppression and racial violence?"

Fletcher tossed the butt of his cigarette into the valley below and walked on in silence, smiling to himself.

Laripa was distinguished among the settlements of the Moroks by the presence of the greatest orator, Malek; the greatest sorcerer, Macardit; and the greatest philosopher, Garang, a twisted, hairless little man with a squint. It was thus a kind of Florence or Paris, a cultural centre where the aspiring young intellectuals of the Moroks came to learn the secrets of their fathers, and, more hidden still, the dark revelations of the Before-Men who, led by Tikame himself, had roamed the mountains when Time itself was not.

As befitted its status as the cultural capital of the Moroks, its men's house was the largest, the best-ornamented, and the most smoke-blackened in all the island. Raised on piles, its rear was low, but the roof-ridge rose into the sky, so that, being more than a hundred feet long, the top of its front end, the formal end, was nearly forty feet above the ground. The boards covering the front of the house were brilliantly painted in the form of a great face, whose mouth was also the entrance. The teeth of this mouth were provided by two rows of bleached skulls, as the boiling and preparation of skulls was one of the arts for which Laripa was celebrated.

Below the men's house, the hovels of the women formed two parallel lines for a couple of hundred yards down the crest of the spur. At the end of these two lines, a second, smaller, men's house faced up the yard between the huts of the women, looking directly at the great face of the principal men's house. The yard was steep and slippery, of shiny red clay, and all around the village ran a high stockade of timbers, whose tops were carved into replicas of simian faces, or barbed to resemble spear points, or hacked and pruned into stranger, even more lethal shapes, curved and twisted like instruments of torture.

The interior of the great men's house was lit only by those rays that penetrated the narrow entrance, and its natural obscurity was rendered the more impenetrable by the smoke which filled it, rising from the smouldering logs on the hearth of ashes running the entire length of the building. Inside the entrance, in the ashes, smoking his bamboo pipe, sat Nyikang, once the most renowned of the Laripa warriors, now little more than an old bag of bones looking out over his beloved mountains, waiting to die.

Smoking was the last of this world's pleasures left to him; the government had stopped most of the axe murders at which he had been so proficient, and he had never been much good at sorcery. He'd always muddled the spells at the critical moment. Sex, well, that had been fun, and at least the government hadn't stopped that yet, but it was a long time since he had felt up to it. The last time, that had been a long time ago, when the great landslide swept away some of his pandanus trees, but all he got for his trouble was a splitting headache, and he had given it up as a bad job ever since. Not that he was missing much as far as Teopo, his last surviving wife, was concerned. She was almost as decrepit as him and never bothered to wash anymore; she was usually covered in dust, like an old gourd abandoned in the corner of a hut.

It was ages, too, since he had led the killing of the pigs at a great dance. His teeth had mostly gone now, and he couldn't even chew a pig, let alone kill one. Soon he would be a spirit, roaming the forests of the high ranges with his ancestors, without fire, or food, or hope. He still clung to life, not out of love of this world, or fear of that to come, but from habit.

His attention wandered back to Macardit and Malek, who were sitting outside on the verandah, talking.

"A bat's wing without fresh dog's blood will blight naught," said Macardit. "Some say that a frog's head, crushed with ginger root, giveth more power than the blood of any creature, but that is folly."

Malek nodded wisely.

"Dog's blood, thou sayest. I will mind it well." His fourth and most recent wife had been seduced by his cousin, so he had come to Macardit for a little private tuition in sorcery. The receipt for smiting an enemy's genitals with gonorrhea cost only a small pig;

a larger one, of course, was required if the Master himself recited the spells. Since this enemy was a cousin, the handier and cheaper remedy of the axe was denied him, but a good dose of the clap would suffice to put the fellow in his place.

"Fresh blood, fresh blood," reiterated Macardit. "If thou but usest fresh blood, the bat's wing, and the words of power which I have given thee, and well besmear his codpiece with the remedy, there will be one pig that will not root in thy garden for a while." Macardit drew on his bamboo pipe, but found that in the long interval of conversation it had died.

"O aged one, give us of thy pipe" he said over his shoulder to Nyikang. Slowly, a trembling arm was extended through the hole with the requested pipe.

The Moroks never addressed an old person by name; they smelt of death, and their names were thus tabooed. Men talked freely in their presence, for they were in a sense unpersons, already dead to the social life around them. But all took care to treat them with respect. The elderly would soon be spirits, and their curses were powerful; no one wanted sudden blindness, or his food to choke him, or his pigs to waste and die.

As the three men smoked in silence, passing the pipe between them, Garang approached. Before climbing the ladder up to the verandah, he blew his nose in his fingers and wiped the snot onto one of the posts supporting the house. When he had settled himself, and drawn a few lungfuls of smoke from the bamboo tube, he said:

"Tikame cometh. We have all heard the bugle. Men say he bringeth an aged one, withered and lean-shanked, who came from the sky."

"Aye. Is it he who was foretold, the bringer of riches?" asked Macardit.

"Who knoweth? We must put him to the test. For if he is that bringer of riches, he is surely one of us, a Morok, returned from the dead, from the great mountains, where the spirits wander for ever. So, my test is this. If there be one among us upon whom he smileth with special favor, like a loving father upon the son in whom he taketh delight, he is that man's begetter, or his sire's begetter, or his grandsire's begetter. For no man smileth in such a fashion upon a stranger, upon any who is not bone of his bone, his very kindred. So if this aged one, this spindle-shanked one, should show love to any of us, love, I say, and not the passing smiles of deceit, he claimeth that one as his very own, and we shall know that he is in truth that bringer of riches foretold by our fathers."

The others, including Nyikang, were deeply impressed by the insight which Garang displayed. The matchless intellect that made Laripa respected and envied throughout all the land of the Moroks seemed only to burn brighter with the years.

"Our men come from the forests with wood, our women from the gardens and creeks. When we are all met together, I shall speak," said Malek, "and reveal thy words, O Garang."

"Aye," said the philosopher. "Strictly charge the men, the women, the wenches and the lads, even the little children, to watch this stranger, to look for the sign. For if it haply pass unseen, or go unrequited, he will be angered, and forsake us, never to return."

Chapter V

AGAINST FLETCHER'S ADVICE, Prout had filled his belly with water at the first stream they came to, so that it slopped and gurgled and made him feel thirstier than ever, draining the little energy he had left. Although it was only half-past two, the sun was heavily clouded over, and the valleys were in deep gloaming. As they drew nearer to their goal Fletcher pointed to Laripa, clearly silhouetted on the ridge across the narrow gorge up which they were moving. In his debilitated state Prout looked across at that menacing skyline, of jagged stockade and crouching, beastlike men's house, with feelings of dread.

His academic success, his professional accomplishments in the service of the underprivileged, even the recent publication of his paper, "The Racist Implications of Air-Conditioning in the Tropics," for which he had been complimented by the Secretary-General in person, did not, in this wild and barbaric land, give quite that boost to morale which a rational man might have expected. He was not looking forward to meeting the Moroks.

As the track penetrated farther into the heart of the gorge, the walls above and below it grew more precipitous, until they were great slabs of rock, in some places overhanging the path, dank, fissured, streaked with green slime where seepages of moisture broke through. The thunder of the torrent at the head of the gorge grew steadily more penetrating and overwhelming, magnified between the encroaching walls of the chasm, while the air grew steadily colder.

When the two men came round a corner a couple of hundred yards from the falls, the noise was deafening, and an icy, clammy wind, carried down by the water in its descent, blew fitfully upon them. A group of police awaited them. Having long since escorted the carriers into the village and setting them to preparing the rest house, some had returned with Cpl Barigi to assist their officer and his guest, and to provide them with a guard of honour for their formal entrance. They were huddled in the lee of a great rock, sheltering from the spray that drifted off the falls, and from this rock there led a native suspension bridge of plaited lawyer vines, that dipped across the gorge in a shallow catenary and rose to a similar anchorage on the opposite side. The bridge was of the simplest construction—two parallel hand-ropes, with a third rope below for the feet, slung from the hand-ropes by thinner vines. To its right, the cataract of the Limilimi thundered into a huge cauldron of black rock, in which great boulders were tossed and spun by the scouring action of the water; their ceaseless rumbling and grinding shook the walls of the gorge, emitting a note so low in register that it was felt rather than heard.

"This is the spot the maries jump from to spite their old men," shouted Fletcher, pointing to the bridge. Beneath it, the tail race from the cauldron flew in a chaos of foam and churning green waters.

"What? Who are the maries?" asked Prout, close to Fletcher's ear.

"The women. Jump over here when they've had a row with their husbands to make 'em feel bad. The police'll show yer how to cross."

The police, who had stood up and given butt salutes with their rifles as Fletcher came up with them, prepared for the crossing. Two constables went first, carrying one end of a light rope. Prout stood in apprehensive misery as he watched the bridge begin to sway through a wider and wider arc with the movements of the two men; slight undulations ran along the vines as they hurried across. When they were safely over, they belayed themselves and Fletcher tied Prout to the middle of the rope.

"OK. Over yer go. Can't fall very far even if the bridge goes!"

All arms and legs, Prout scrabbled and floundered between the vines. Like a spastic spider, thought Fletcher, as he paid out the safety line. After about five minutes the piteous exhibition was over, and the remaining police crossed, followed by Fletcher and Cpl Barigi, who both made a careful examination of the vines on their way. Now only a short, but steep, climb lay between them and the village, and in another quarter of an hour they had surmounted this final obstacle. Their progress did not go unobserved, however, and the forest around them was alive with the shrieks and laughs of naked urchins who peered out, round eyed, at the strange red man of whom their elders had been talking, then ran off giggling and chattering.

At last the trees thinned out, and gave way to scantier vegetation of sword-grass, bushes, and casuarina trees. Signs of former cultivation became more obvious, and soon they were walking past newly planted gardens of sweet potato, taro, and sugar cane, surrounded by stout timber fences against the ravages of the village pigs. Ahead of them a square house, raised on piles, came into view over the fences. As the party reached it the notes of a bugle rang out, blown by one of the constables who had remained behind at the rest house with Sgt Oala. In front of the rest house, on the wide expanse of grass, maintaining a deathly silence, was the assembled population of Laripa, with Malek, their chief, and other notables at the salute in front. The police formed in line before the flagpole, facing the crowd, and presented arms as the Australian flag was slowly raised, to the accompaniment of the bugle. Just as it reached the head of the pole, ready to be broken out, a large pig dashed from the crowd making for the forest. Fletcher drew his Webley .45, fired, and bowled it over with a single massive slug in the ribs.

Prout, standing beside Fletcher in front of the police, was stunned. "You sadistic thug," he muttered to himself. He knew that if he didn't immediately make some public act of solidarity with these wretched people, his mission would be permanently discredited by its association with the appalling Fletcher. Just as he was meditating some decisive gesture, however, Fletcher stepped forward to address the crowd.

"So, my people, I have come. And with me I bring an elder of my tribe, who loveth you well. But though he loveth you, he knoweth not your ways, nor yet your tongue; in these matters, though old in years, he is but a little child, grasping beyond his reach, prattling of things beyond his understanding. Bear with him, then, and mind ye well that he liveth under my protection. Smile upon him, and he will reward you; deal kindly with him, and he will shower you with riches. I have spoken."

As Fletcher concluded his address, which was embellished with many of the rhetorical flourishes beloved by the Moroks, but which are too tedious to be repeated here, a babble of talk broke out among the people. Malek silenced it with a sweep of his arm as he stepped forward.

"O Tikame! Thy words bring gladness to thy people of Laripa. Thy presence alone warmeth our bellies; our women are happy, our children are happy, our dogs are happy, our pigs are happy..." his eloquence faltered slightly, "...our happiness is like unto the waters of the Limilimi, that falleth from Mount Karama without ceasing." A great burst of applause greeted this unusually fine allegory. He allowed it to die away. "And this, the elder of thy people; let him come among us as one of our true kinsmen. Our women shall cram his mouth with taro; the juice of our sugar cane shall sweeten his lips; the fat of our pigs shall run down his chin, so that his breast may shine in the firelight. When his shadow falleth upon our pigs, they shall wax fat; when it falleth upon our women, their wombs shall be heavy; when it falleth upon the ground of our fathers, it shall yield taro, and sweet-potatoes, and yams, and cucumbers, in abundance; and when it falleth upon our old men, they shall grow young. I have spoken."

The applause at the conclusion of this impassioned harangue was tremendous, and while it continued Fletcher turned to Prout.

"I gave 'em the good oil, about how yer were a mate of mine and came up here to hand out some goodies. The chief says he and his folks'll treat yer like one o' themselves. So if yer give 'em some tobacco and newspaper they'll love yer like a brother."

"Yes, well, the sooner I establish decent relations with these people the better. After your sickening treatment of that poor pig, God knows what they'll think of me."

"It's a chief's privilege to kill any animal that interrupts him during a speech—they do the same themselves, you'll learn."

"I didn't come here to learn that kind of thing. I came here to help, and one doesn't help people by encouraging their worst behaviour."

"I'll have the tobacco and paper dug out for yer."

"Not yet. There's something I have to do first."

Prout turned away, with the first sense of satisfaction he had felt since the morning, and hobbled over to the rest house, and climbed the steps to the verandah. The house was solidly made, the walls and floor of pandanus bark, and the roof thatched with leaves from the same tree. Inside was a large room with two beds, each formed by running a couple of poles through a tube of canvas, and lashing them to cross-pieces wedged against the walls at each end. Two folding chairs were the only other furniture. The patrol boxes and other gear were stacked inside, and Cpl Barigi was busy extracting cooking pots and billies for tea.

In a connecting room, some carriers were blowing a fire, made on a hearth of mud and stones, into a blaze. Another house for the police, with a kitchen, was close to the rest house, and the smoke from the two fires was warm and comforting, since the afternoon mist was already drifting around them, dank and chilly from the mountain above.

Prout went over to the piled baggage and picked up his ruck-sack. After fumbling inside for a few moments, he withdrew a wad of banknotes, in Australian currency, and took it outside onto the verandah. Fletcher was standing below, making arrangements for guard duty with Sgt Oala.

"Could I please speak to the carriers?" said Prout. Fletcher sighed. What did he want now? He shouted for the carriers to line up. When they had assembled, and stood gazing at Prout with in-different eyes, Prout called the first one up the verandah steps, and held out a handful of notes.

"There, my friend. That's for all your hard work of today in carrying my bag." He gestured to his back, and pointed to his bag, which he had thrown on the verandah. The man grasped his meaning instantly, and seizing the money with a grin skipped down the steps and ran off to the police house. The other carriers, now keenly interested, clustered round the steps, and the same perfor-mance was repeated, accompanied by hilarious laughter from the carriers. Fletcher and Sgt Oala watched in astonishment as the Lar-ipa people gathered closer. When the last of the carriers had received his money, Prout felt relieved.

"Now," he said, hobbling down the steps again, "we can settle the matter of the pig." He made his way painfully to where the pig lay on its side in the grass.

"Ask them, please, whose pig this is. I want to compensate the owner."

Fletcher translated the question, with the smiling indulgence normally reserved for small children. Sensing his contempt for Prout, the Moroks all began claiming the pig and pressed forward clamorously, each determined to get his hands on the reward. Men tapped their chests peremptorily and scowled, or pushed forward their copiously weeping womenfolk who were holding out their hands in supplication. Prout was taken aback by the flood of savages, whom he was seeing for the first time at close quarters, and in panic began thrusting bundles of notes into their hands, quailing inwardly under the gaze of their burning eyes.

They examined the notes suspiciously; they knew coins, but had scarcely seen banknotes before, and considered them extremely inferior substitutes for the half-sheets of newspaper which Fletcher gave them when he was in a good mood. Tobacco was the traditional gift of a chief. Frowning, the men rolled the notes experimentally between their fingers, to test their value for cigarettes, and found them hard, shiny, and thoroughly unsatisfactory. Children, in the arms of their fathers, reached for the notes, and pressed them to their snotty noses, crumpled them, smeared their faces with them, and, losing interest, allowed them to drop heedlessly into the mud around them. The women snatched them for closer inspection, but, discovering that both sides were green, a color which ranked at the bottom in their scale of preferences for personal decoration, tossed them away into the wind.

As their murmuring grew into a clamour of irritation and bewilderment, Prout began to realise that his scheme was going wrong.

"Money, money!" he began shouting, pointing at the notes, sweat running down his face as he beamed and gesticulated.

"Moni, moni," repeated dozens of voices, a vague recognition slowly dawning. Some of the carriers, hearing the commotion, came out from the kitchen and began explaining the significance of these bits of paper. The scowling brows and angry gestures were soon replaced by smiles and laughter, and Prout was besieged by clutching hands and soon relieved of the rest of his stock. Laughing and exhilarated, he walked slowly back to the rest house, through the press of his new friends. He regarded Fletcher with a look of triumph:

"Well, you see, one doesn't have to be a linguist to express oneself. The basic language of humanity is the outstretched hand of friendship."

"Outstretched hand of bludging, more like. If yer think yer can buy these bastards off with a few quid, ye've got another think coming. The only thing these jokers understand is bayonets and a belt round the ear. Still, as long as ye're enjoyin' yerself…"

"I thought you'd take that attitude. You'll just have to get used to the idea that kindness and compassion leave a more lasting impression than fear and violence." His eyes left Fletcher's face, and wandered over the village, the spur, and the great valley. "This is the first time someone has come here and shown them sympathy and behaved with human understanding. You wouldn't understand that. All you can do is terrify and brutalize."

He looked challengingly at Fletcher, whose contemptuous smile did not waver. "I see it's no use trying to argue with you. I should like to see the village. Perhaps you will come with me as an interpreter?"

Fletcher, still smiling, nodded his acquiescence.

After tea they took the path that led down from the rest house, with the men of Laripa clustering round, Malek and his friends closest of all. As they drew near the stockade an odour of human faeces, which had been discernible near the rest house, became pungent and obtrusive.

"Why don't you make them dig proper latrines?"

"What's the point? The pigs and dogs lap up most of it, and it's well clear of the drinking places. They don't like the taste of shit in their drinking water any more'n yer do."

"It's still disgusting. As soon as I return from Rabaul it's the first thing I'll have done."

By now they had reached the entrance to the stockade, where a few timbers had been uprooted and were lying cast aside in the bushes. Prout looked up at the hideous, cruel carvings on the posts with respectful interest. Clearly, people who were so dexterous with their hands had great potential as mechanics and clerks in the modern society he was planning for them. He was less impressed by the two lines of dismal hovels that flanked the yard, which was scattered with pig droppings.

"It's no wonder their behaviour is sometimes violent, when they live in surroundings like this. It's well established that environmental disadvantages of this type can lead to anti-social behaviour. What they need is piped water, model houses, cottage industry, and sanitation. And it only needs the *will*, I assure you. They will respond eagerly enough. Of course, a social democracy needs an elected assembly, people's courts, and a trade union movement, but such things can be built up rather more quickly than one might imagine. There's promise here, I can see it. Now, what's that extraordinary building?" he asked, as he caught sight of the men's house.

"That's the club, the men's house. No women allowed."

"No women? My wife will want to change all that! Still, we mustn't rush things, especially when there are so many other projects to keep us busy. I should like to have a look inside."

He climbed up onto the verandah, assisted by Malek and Macardit, who crawled inside and helped Prout through the narrow entrance. Fletcher elected to remain outside. No sooner were they in
the club than Malek blew on the fire, while Macardit took down
some smoked pandanus nuts from a shelf above the hearth. He began cracking them between two stones, and offering the interiors to
Prout. The kernels were dry, yet oily, faintly kipper-flavored, but
quite pleasant. Prout munched busily and began to look about him,
but the interior was even darker than it had been in the morning
because of the heavy cloud and mist, and for a time he could discern
very little. But as the fire began to blaze up he became aware of a
corpse huddled on the floor, covered in a layer of ashes.

"Fletcher! There's a dead body in here!"

"Unlikely. Dead bodies go in the women's houses until they're
buried. It's probably some old git havin' a kip."

"Ask these men who he is, will you?"

Fletcher did so. Macardit gave the corpse a prod with the stone
he was using to crack the nuts. It was Nyikang; the old man stirred,
rolled over and accumulated more ashes in doing so, and heaved
himself into a sitting position; his eyes were gummed together with
the mucus of sleep and his chest was covered with scabs, which had
been smeared with clay. He looked like Lazarus released from the
tomb. Prout watched, open-mouthed with horror, as the apparition
rubbed its eyes with its knuckles and fixed him with its bloodshot
gaze.

"They say his name's Nyikang, and that he will die soon because
he is very old."

"Poor old man. Poor, poor old man." Prout was deeply moved.
To die like this, filthy, naked, diseased, infirm, when he should have
been given the loving care of his family to soothe his last days on
earth, or, better still, been placed in a municipal home for the aged.

Impulsively, he reached out both hands to the old man and took his bony old claws in a warm grip. He gazed into the aged one's eyes, and smiled.

Nyikang, recovering his wits, grinned with toothless gums, and disengaging a hand from Prout's sympathetic clasp, reached into a gourd behind him and brought out a small piece of mouldy dried tobacco leaf which he offered to Prout, hoping for a present in return. Prout took it and recalled that he had a packet of cigarettes in his shirt pocket. They were rather crushed, but still smokeable. He gave the whole packet to Nyikang.

Macardit and Malek exchanged glances. The old man turned the packet over, inspecting it carefully in the firelight, but his curved, blackened finger nails could make no impression on the cellophane, until finally Prout reached over to strip the packet, took out a cigarette, and put it between Nyikang's lips. Then he lit it for him with his lighter. The old man puffed ecstatically, and Prout watched him with a benign smile. At last he got up to go, clutching the mouldy leaf of tobacco.

"Tell them," he said to Fletcher, "that I like this man very much. He is my good friend." Fletcher dutifully complied.

Dusk was falling as Prout crawled out of the men's house, and the evening mists had risen from the river gorge to blanket the village. The people who had gathered outside the men's house called out gaily to the two men as they made their way out of the village and up the track to the rest house, where they were greeted with curried bully-beef and rice, hot tea and rum, to keep out the cold of the night.

As they finished their silent meal, spread out on the tops of patrol boxes, Fletcher cocked his ear to listen to the conversation of the carriers in the kitchen, where they were boiling water to wash up.

"They're callin' yer Father of Nyikang," he said. "Wouldn't surprise me if they reckoned you were his *real* father, come back from
the dead!"

"Oh, please! Can you not simply admit that there is such a thing
as genuine human sympathy, without any superstitious mumbo-
jumbo attached, and that they responded to it?"

"Suit yerself, mate. I was only thinkin' aloud." Fletcher poured
himself another glass of rum and drew deeply on his cigarette. The
rain had been falling for some time, and was now battering on the
roof. But there was a good fire in the kitchen; this was one of the
better rest houses on the island. There were no leaks anywhere, the
pressure lantern was hissing smoothly, and most importantly, there
was another bottle of Neghrita Rhum in his patrol box. Fletcher felt
that even a lecture on human rights could not spoil the pleasure of
an evening like this, relaxing after a good day's march, warm, dry,
and full of grub, with a glass of grog, listening to the rain. All he
needed now was an obliging young mary.

"What did yer think of the skulls?"

"Skulls? I didn't see any skulls."

"You bloody intellectuals are all the same. Only see what the
books tell yer to see, don't yer?"

"You don't have much time for books, do you, Fletcher?"

"Too right, I don't. That's the trouble with the world today. As
Olly's always sayin', all books and no brains."

Prout frowned.

"That's the kind of glib generalisation that makes our work ten
times harder. How do you think we can begin to solve the urgent
social problems of our time without a thorough scientific understanding of the way pre-modern societies function? For that we need
books, in order to communicate our data and what we have learned

in the course of our research. Doctors need books, but you don't condemn them for that!"

"Yeah, but yer don't go to the quack unless yer feelin' crook. No one's grumblin' on this island. You bastards make up the diseases as yer go along, and then try to con us ye're the only blokes with the right medicines. Sod that for a racket."

"But you can't be oblivious to the urgent personal problems here, the squalor, the—"

"Listen, mate, I've got an urgent personal problem, and I'm buggered if *you* can solve it. See yer in the mornin'."

It was some time before Prout realised where Fletcher had gone.

In the morning, Prout could hardly bear to squeeze his blistered feet into his cold, sodden boots. Fletcher came strolling up through the soaking grass from the village, looking well pleased with himself. As the two were breakfasting in silence, Sgt Oala entered the house in some alarm. The carriers were refusing to move until they were paid in advance for each item of baggage.

"I think that's quite reasonable," said Prout, "After all, in a just society, one can't expect them to carry for nothing. I'll get some money."

"Ye're as silly as a bag full of arseholes, aren't yer? If yer give 'em what they're after, they'll double the price tomorrer, and double it again the next day. In the end yer'll be payin' so flamin', much it'll be cheaper to bring blokes over from England to move our gear."

"I'm in charge here, Fletcher!"

"Yer a pain in the arse. I'll handle this. Sergeant, what name man make him big fellow trouble?"

"Kokoti, sah."

"Oh yeah, Snail Slime. I know the bastard. Raus him Kokoti long house kiap."

"Yessah."

A few parents, who had lost a number of children, chose names for their newborns that were intended to deceive the evil spirits and convince them that the bearers of those names were so contemptible that it was not worth the trouble of maiming them, or covering them in pustules. Fortunately, the malice of the spirits was exceeded only by their stupidity, so this religious camouflage was surprisingly effective.

Kokoti, or Snail Slime, as his name translates into English, appeared beneath the verandah, with his mates a few yards behind him to back him up. Behind them were the police. Kokoti was unusually narrow-featured for a Morok, with permanently half-closed eyes, and a small moustache that had been inspired by a scrap of magazine in the gaol featuring Douglas Fairbanks, the Younger. Kokoti gazed up at Fletcher, insolently, with folded arms.

"Jeez, I must be losin' me grip," thought Fletcher as he came nonchalantly down the steps. As he reached the bottom he smiled at Snail Slime, and hooked a smashing blow into his jaw. Snail Slime landed on his back in the grass, not moving. There was a hiss of indrawn breath from his companions. Fletcher walked over and checked to confirm that Kokoti was unconscious. Only then did he look up from the body of the fallen man into the eyes of each carrier in turn. He held out his hand, and curtly demanded the money which Prout had given them. They all fumbled in the belts of their laplaps and produced the now-soiled notes they had been given the day before.

When he had collected all the money, he dismissed them, shaken and furtive, and went back inside the rest house, after detailing Sgt Oala to fetch three replacement carriers from the village, and to have a pole cut on which to suspend Kokoti for the journey back to Ungabunga.

Prout, who had witnessed the over-ruling of Snail Slime, was crouched by a patrol box, his head in his hands. He raised a stricken face as Fletcher entered.

"For God's sake get me a drink, Fletcher. I can't take any more of this, I just can't."

Fletcher pulled the unopened bottle of rum from a patrol box and poured a stiff drink for Prout, and took a good swig himself, to celebrate a job well done.

"It's my feet as well. I can hardly walk. I don't think I could last another two days."

"Feelin' a bit crook, are yer? Yeah, well, it's a bit rough at first. We'd better pack it in. If we leave now we'll be back by tea time, easy. Here's yer money back, by the way. Wouldn't want yer to think I nicked it."

Prout pocketed the roll of notes.

"It's not their fault, it's not their fault," he said, brokenly. "You've made them like wild animals, who have to snatch everything they can today for fear of what tomorrow may bring."

Fletcher didn't bother to argue, but simply gave a short laugh and began giving orders to the police and carriers to assemble the gear. Prout stood alone on the verandah, keeping out of the way of the busy men. A number of the Laripa people came to see the patrol off, hoping for another handout of money, but when they realised none was forthcoming they soon drifted away. As the patrol moved out, only Malek, by virtue of his rank as Village Constable, was still there to see them go, standing stiffly at the salute. Garang also watched, but from the cover of the trees.

Chapter VI

THE ELEVENTH SKY VAN of the week touched down at Ungabunga, heavy with the necessities of life which a compassionate world showers upon its underprivileged brethren, including one hundred plastic Japanese clarinets and all the other instruments required for a full orchestra from UNESCO for the Department of Cultural Development; thirty-five gross of ceramic ashtrays, each with the blue emblem of the United Nations in the centre to spread the message of international peace among the Moroks; a social science library of seven thousand volumes for the use of the Mission; boxes of French letters and plastic models of the genitalia for the sex education clinic; bales of flags and bunting to encourage national pride; almost two miles of educational film strip, including such basic masterpieces as "The Nude," and "From Leyden Jar to Fusion Reactor"; and a prefabricated gymnasium for Morok children, intended to correct defects of posture, from UNICEF. The custody of the gymnasium was the subject of bitter dispute between the Department of Health and the Department of Community Harmony.

As the aircraft taxied to a halt and began to lower its cargo ramp, a horde of young Morok men, dressed in blue shorts and blue United Nations t-shirts provided free by that generous organisation, dashed forward to begin unloading it. At first they had eagerly pillaged the cargoes, putting the contents to uses which would have amazed and disconcerted their makers, but by now even their prodigious capacity for parodying the treasures of Western civilisation had become dulled by the increasing eccentricity of the cargoes, so they did no more than tentatively finger the crates and bales, awed by their profusion and by their mystery.

When the first Sky Van had arrived, six weeks after Prout's pilgrimage to Laripa, the police had been prepared to deal with looting by their customary techniques of bruising the culprits' toes with rifle butts, or making them run up and down the strip carrying heavy weights above their heads, but Prout would not hear of any such punitive measures.

"We must expect a little pilfering at first," he had retorted to Fletcher's expostulations, as fifty Moroks capered insanely about the runway in bonnets fashioned from maternity brassieres. "Having been deprived of their rights for so long, it's quite natural for them to be a little exuberant when they are permitted to exercise them for the first time. But the only true discipline is self-discipline. It may take a while to take root, but it is all the more lasting for it."

The two men were standing in what had previously been the Government HQ, but was now the Logistics and Supply Centre, of which Oelrichs was, for the time being, in control. While Fletcher and Prout argued, he was leafing through the cargo manifests for the first twelve loads. During a lull in their dispute, he looked up and said:

"If I may say so, there are some items on these lists which don't seem urgently needed for the time being. There are lawn-mowers, four dozen of them, in cargo three, for example."

"No, no, Mr. Oelrichs, there you're quite mistaken, I'm afraid, quite mistaken. (The theory of social change was one of Prout's favorite topics.) You see, the great fallacy of arguments like that is to believe that because these sorts of items have no *immediate* use, they are unneccessary and absurd. In fact, these items you mention have been most carefully selected by experts. Now, of course, I agree that today, this minute, lawn mowers would be rather difficult to operate in most villages, and would perhaps not achieve very useful results, but that's not the point. It's only when the people see these things that they will realise their uses, and will eventually want to re-order their lives and roles around them. What to you are frivolous and unnecessary luxuries out here, to me, and other theorists of social change, are essential catalysts in stimulating a restructuring of need-awareness. Or, in layperson's terms, the people can only be induced to accept change of their own free will if they are made dissatisfied with their old lifestyle, and the only way we can do that is to give them concrete examples of a new and better one. As you both become better acquainted with modern techniques of inducing social change, you will realise that it is essential to produce dissatisfaction, resentment, even envy, in the early stages of a project like this; after all, envy may be sneered at by those inclined towards religion and superstition, but regarded rationally, it is basic to material progress. In fact, I don't know where we'd be without it, since without envy, or at least dissatisfaction, we couldn't have change, and then everything would just go on as it had always done, which would be absurd, of course."

During the weeks that followed, the Sky Vans delivered, in addition to their other cargo, the prefabricated sections for the new buildings at Ungabunga, which were swiftly erected by crews of Tolai, from Rabaul, so that in a miraculously short space of time, Ungabunga was carpeted in a maze of asbestos-walled bungalows, offices, store-sheds, display-centres and conference-rooms. But the fort remained on its hill, overlooking all, as a reminder of the old order.

One afternoon, an earnest conference was held in Hut 27 on the subject of this odious survival of reaction. Prout was seated in his chair, flanked by his wife Phyllis, a fleshy blonde, her hair wreathed round her head in a thick plait, who was acting as his secretary, and by Joe Treadwell, seconded from the South Thames Gas Board to be the Secretary for Energy and Trade Unionism. The deep purple of his countenance hinted that, apart from wearing an ill-fitting collar, prodigious forces for social good were in imminent danger of eruption. But his mates back home knew that a state of permanent frustration with his better half, Mabel Treadwell, also had a great deal to do with it, and that it was as much to escape from her as any feeling of sympathy for the Third World, that he had come to Elephant Island. This was the first such assignment he had been on, and he felt, in his antipodean isolation, as though the responsibility for defending the reputations of the whole British Trade Union Movement and the Gas Board in particular against devious and unappreciative foreigners rested on his shoulders alone.

He also took great pains to conceal the fact that his middle name was Obadiah.

To his right sat Rebeccah Bloom, from New York, the Secretary for Political Consciousness, sallow-faced and biting her nails, and opposite her was the Ecological Efficiency Officer, Tristram Daubeny, who as well as being golden-haired and pinkly handsome, had been afflicted with the additional disadvantage, in that company, of being independently wealthy. At the end of the table was an empty chair which should have been filled by Michael Moncreif, lawyer and constitutional draftsman, who was unaccountably delayed in arriving from Port Moresby.

"Can't think why you didn't clear the 'ole ruddy lot out when you first came, Sid," said Treadwell. "Give 'em their marching orders and no messing about. Bloody little 'itlers they are."

"That Oelrichs makes me *sick*," interjected Rebeccah, drawing down her thick lower lip, and dilating her nostrils in disgust. "Just *sick*. Those poor indigenes actually had to *carry* the fat creepy bastard around in some goddamn throne. Just outa' this world."

Prout raised a pacificatory hand.

"I quite understand your sense of outrage at the goings-on here. Having seen Fletcher in action during my tour of inspection, I'm probably even more disgusted than any of you. But we can't just get rid of them on the spot. To begin with, Fletcher and Oelrichs know the people and the language, so for a few months, until we establish our own relationship with the people, we need their knowledge. But there is an even more important reason for keeping them here. I must ask you to keep this strictly confidential for the time being."

His audience hung on every word, as he told them of his unexpected discovery that, despite the frequency of every other kind of violence, no homicides had been reported on the island.

"When I pointed out this curious anomaly to Oelrichs, he just smiled, and said, 'That's surely a compliment, Dr. Prout. Our methods may not be orthodox, but they seem to be fairly effective. Surely you can't hold *that* against us as well?' He seemed almost to be expecting the question. Perhaps I should have said nothing. However, on the plane back to Rabaul after my first visit, the pilot let slip one remark which was rather interesting. I said that it was our policy to have a resident legal officer, in such cases as Elephant Island, and he replied, something like 'Fletcher would never have that. Can't stand judges nosing about the place.' What I'm getting at is that there have almost *certainly* been homicides here among the indigenous people, and that Fletcher and his police have taken the law into their own hands by removing them from the records. I suspect that instead of imposing the moderate prison sentence that Canberra allows, they have callously slaughtered those they believed responsible. However, once the people realise that Fletcher is now powerless, I don't think it will take us long to persuade someone to come forward, and then we'll have the lot of them."

"The dirty bastards oughta be exterminated," burst out Rebeccah. "Cut their friggin' nuts off!"

"Well, I don't think we can quite go that far, although I tend to share your sentiments."

"Fair enough, Sid, we're lumbered with 'em until you can pin charges on 'em, but what about this bloody fortress contraption, and them thugs with swords and 'elmets? You aren't goin' to let *them* go on rampagin' around bashin' the people, are you?"

"I was coming to that, Joe. If we do nothing else, the destruction of the fort will make it quite clear to the people what our intentions are, and that we mean business. We can ask for volunteers from the local villages to tear it down. As for the police, I have already made an order forbidding further patrolling, unless the patrol is directed by a member of my staff. In the future, no weapons of any description will be carried. U.N. uniforms are to be worn, of course. Handcuffs are to be abolished. Arrests will take place only with the consent of the person being arrested. That should remove the problem of the police for the time being. As for the gaol, that will be destroyed together with the fortress, and Ungabunga will be declared a Zone of Custodial Care; within which, indigenous persons—and Europeans, of course—who are the subject of a Care Order will be placed on parole not to go beyond the Zone boundary without permission, except at weekends, or for compassionate reasons, or when deemed under the domination of an irresistible impulse."

The others nodded their heads.

"These are obviously such basic remedies, the kind that we have to make at the very beginning of our programme, before we can contemplate anything more ambitious. Do we need to discuss them? No? Good."

"While we're on the subject of the fort," said Treadwell, "maybe it'd be in order for me to ask if any proposals 'ave been made for the utilisation of the site."

"Do you have any suggestions?"

"Well, as Secretary for Energy, it's my duty to draw the attention of this committee to the need to install a power source without delay. There are only two sources of power that concern us, electricity and gas. If we generate our own electricity, apart from the cost of the fuel, we 'ave the capital cost of the generating plant, and the problem of skilled maintenance, and so on. Now, if we 'ave gas, the only capital equipment we need is of a very simple sort: storage tanks, reduction valves, and basic piping, all cheap enough. Domestic fittings work out about the same whether it's gas or electricity. Maintenance of a gas storage depot will need fitters, of course, but I can train 'em meself—should be able to, thirty-five years in the trade and the Union, started me apprenticeship at fourteen!"

He laughed, but he was the only one.

"What chances are there for hydro-electric power?" asked Prout.

"Given time, it might be promising, but there's no feasibility study, no met'rological data. That'd take several years, and no use asking Fletcher and that gang. We'd look right Charlies if we stuck an intake pipe in some stream and the bloody thing dried up on us six months later, eh? So for my money, it's gas all the time."

"That all seems very well thought-out, Joe. I can't see any objections at the moment. We obviously have to import some sort of fuel, whether it is diesel or gas. Yes, a very good scheme, Joe."

"But y'know, Sid, there's more to gas than that, much more. If we 'ad electricity, I doubt if even I could train the local people to maintain the equipment and appliances. We'd 'ave to rely on expats, which we must avoid at all costs. So by usin' gas, we train up bright young lads into the trade, and lay the foundations of the Trade Union movement 'ere, into the bargain. And I don't need to expand on what it would mean for the people to 'ave a flourishing Trade Union movement." There was a chorus of agreement. "And where better to put the Ungabunga Gas Works than in the same place where their oppressors 'ave 'eld sway for God knows 'ow many years? Answer me that!"

He sat back in his chair, more purple than ever, and pulled a handkerchief from his trousers to mop his brow.

"Your idea is brilliant, Joe," Prout said eagerly. "It's a wonderful example of what the whole philosophy of our mission should be. This is the use of modern technology as the driving force to convince the people to accept rational, modern social institutions, such as your trade unions. Absolutely first-class. Would it be possible to extend the services of the gas works into the surrounding areas?"

Treadwell nodded vigorously.

"Bad housing is one aspect of the traditional approach to life that we must root out here, but the arduous nature of indigenous cooking must be another. Imagine having to heat a pile of stones over blazing logs and then bury them in the ground before you can even have a little roast pork! Just think what it would mean for the outlook of these people to have neat modern houses, and be able to cook their meals over gas rings!"

"That's crap," snarled Rebeccah, "Only you Brits could be crazy enough to come up with an idea like *gas*! Who ever heard of gas? Let 'em have electricity like everyone else, for Christ's sake!"

"We've already been over the social and technological implications of electricity, Rebeccah," said Prout. "I thought the advantages of gas as a source of power were obvious to all of us."

"Yeah, yeah, I know. I'm only a dumb female. Gotta leave all that technology to those big male intellects. Wake me up when ya' get to the babies' bottles and diapers."

After an uneasy pause, Treadwell said:

"I see no reason why gas shouldn't be able to provide an extensive service in outlying villages. We'll be able to have sub-stations in the villages themselves. Get the cylinders charged at Ungabunga."

"True. Well, lets take that as settled. We'll have the fort destroyed as soon as possible, and set up your gas works there as soon as the equipment can be flown in," said Prout. "Now, there are one or two other matters to address. Latrines, number one. When I was on my patrol, I was disgusted by the lack of any regulations for the disposal of human waste. Here again, we must use an improvement in the people's material conditions of life as part of our drive to develop rational attitudes to social reforms. I think the obvious person to instruct the people in the digging of latrines would be Dr. Smith. I'll have him go out on a patrol and explain the necessity of sanitation. There seem to be a few shovels in the villages, so there should be no problem about digging them. Now, Tristram, what was this about traps?"

"Oh, er, yes, Dr Prout," said Daubeny. "Well, I've been looking around a bit, I mean, not like you, right up in the mountains, but at the people here, and it seems that they are a bit undernourished. It's rather difficult to say for sure."

"Oh, do get on with it, lad, or we'll be 'ere till tea time," laughed Treadwell.

"Well, I'm trying to. What I'm getting at is that they seem to be short of protein in their diet, and I was wondering if we couldn't help them to catch game and so on in the forests. There must be plenty there. What made me think of it was seeing all those boxes of gin traps in the Number 2 warehouse. If we gave them to the people, they'd be marvellous for helping them obtain more protein in their diet. But, er, perhaps you'd already thought of that, or wanted them for something else?" He looked more confused and embarrassed by his own words than by Treadwell's impatience.

"I think, to be honest, Tristram, that the traps you mention came here due to an oversight on someone's part. Oelrichs and I were wondering what to do with them. You've solved that for us. If you like you can arrange the distribution of them yourself. It'll help you get to know the people."

"That would be absolutely wonderful!"

"Good. Now we come to the issue of education. As you know, Fletcher has done nothing whatever to promote schooling in all the years he has been here, and I know that Tristram and Rebeccah are particularly concerned—"

"Yes," broke in Tristram, "Surely, since we are going to be learning Pidgin we could at least have some classes for the people in that."

Prout winced.

"Please, Tristram, try not to use old colonialist terms like 'Pidgin'. The correct name is Neo-Melanesian. These little details matter, you know."

Tristram looked suitably embarrassed, but Rebeccah interrupted.

"Ya' can call it what ya' like, but it's still a shitty language. The people have a goddam right to learn English."

"I totally agree," said Treadwell.

Prout raised both his hands to silence them.

"I quite understand your feelings," he said, "but there is a basic issue of principle here which must take precedence over everything else. We must not assume that when the people attain independence, they will necessarily *want* to learn English, because that has profound political implications. They may wish to become non-aligned and learn Swahili, or possibly Esperanto, or even French. We really *must* respect their human rights in this and leave them to take their own decision as a sovereign people at independence!"

While the meeting dragged on, the cargo handlers getting the last crates from the plane were astonished to find, in a nook behind the pilot's cabin, a sleeping constitutional lawyer, reeking of wine. After a few minutes, aroused by their babble, albeit deferential babble, he opened an eye and surveyed them.

"I presume you are not the President and his cabinet come to welcome me, since I haven't invented them yet. So I'll assume that you're harmless porter chappies, and disemplane accordingly. Toodle-oo!" He smiled broadly on them, picked up his chianti bottle and clapped a wide straw hat on his head, covering the mass of brilliant red hair that glowed like a blaze in a distillery. Followed by the goggling eyes of the natives, he ambled up the edge of the strip until he spotted the pub. Reaching the bridge over the drainage ditch, he sauntered over to where Fletcher and Oakley were standing by the door.

"Good afternoon to you. Can I get a refill here?"

"G'day. I dare say there's a drop inside, let's go and see. I'm Roger Fletcher, by the way, and this is Ned Oakley." They turned to go inside.

"How do you do. Michael Moncreif. Aren't you the Resident Magistrate?"

"Yeah. What's yer line?"

"Oh, I'm the Destroying Angel, as far as you're concerned, I'm afraid. Come to sweep you into oblivion with a stroke of my pen. I'm drafting the new constitution."

"The new what?" They had reached the bar, and Fletcher called for beers all round. "What did yer say yer were?" he repeated.

"I'm a lawyer, constitutional draftsman. Come to draw up the new constitution. Though from what I've seen of the inhabitants of Elephant Island so far, if you gave them the vote, they'd stick the ballot papers up each other's bottoms. Cheers!"

"Cheers!" For a few minutes only the gurgle of ice-cold lagers from stubbies into parched throats broke the silence, until Moncreif addressed them.

"Have you met my colleagues? I suppose you must have done. God! aren't they a shower?"

"Speakin' for myself, the biggest load of no-hopers I ever clapped eyes on," said Oakley. "How did such a reasonable feller like yerself get mixed up with 'em?"

"Hundred thousand dollars a year, tax-free. Unlimited booze, unlimited screwing. Who wouldn't? To be fair, these constitutions I write are absolute cock, but since none of the little charmers they're written for can understand a word of them, I don't suppose they do much harm. This one'll be a two-chamber legislature job, unless I'm much mistaken. Sounds like privy-building, doesn't it? I did have some notes on what they wanted, but I must have dropped them at the airport. Never mind, get them tomorrow from old Snout, or whatever he calls himself."

"There's a conference been going on all afternoon."

"Oh, sod them and their conferences. My turn for a round."

That evening, and several crates of stubbies later, Moncreif accepted his old mate Fletcher's invitation to come up and live at his residence, to which both men were shortly carried by the police, singing a regimental lullaby.

Chapter VII

THE PATH FROM LARIPA would have taken Prout still deeper and higher into the mountains, to Dolivi, which controlled the pass at the head of the Loma valley. Here one spur of Mount Wordsworth joined another of Mount Shakespeare, or Karama, as the Moroks knew it, and on either side of this watershed gushed the headwaters of the Ungabunga and the Loma rivers. The pass, at about eight thousand feet, was submerged in the gloomy luxuriance of the ancient forest, but the government road, combined with landslides, had thinned some of the vegetation, so that it was just possible, through a screen of trailing vines, and the spiky, mop-like heads of young pandanus trees, and the giant ferns, to gaze out beyond the forest on either side.

On the Ungabunga side, through breaks in the ranges, could be distantly glimpsed the sea, hardly separable from the sky. The Arafura Sea, which none of the mountain men had ever seen up close, was as remote from their experience, and as mythical, as the surface of the moon. On the Loma side the view was more constricted. The torrent which was to become the Loma took a crooked, cloistered course from the very beginning, winding down a narrow valley which turned at right angles to the pass after only three miles, blocking a watcher's view with the twelve-thousand foot mass of Mount Shakespeare. This was a closed valley, closed to the sun, which only illuminated it in the hours around noon; closed to the winds; and closed to the sight and sound of other villages. Even the pin-point lights of their fires could not be glimpsed in the darkness, and the wailing cries by which the Moroks of the valleys called to one another were blocked by some trick of acoustics from penetrating here. Only the rain fell in vertical abundance, and the mists and dank airs rolled down from the high peaks to blanket the valley of the Dolivi men at nightfall.

The village of Dolivi stood a few hundred feet below the head of the pass, on a flat place close to the torrent. It was usually an undistinguished group of hovels, with the standard men's house and stockade, but it was now, despite the gloom of its setting, trans-formed into a festive arena. The squalid old huts had been cleared away, and replaced by two lines of imposing dwellings, still made from dried pandanus-palm leaf, but of leaves that were crisp and shiny, and golden brown, instead of the limp, bleached things that had coated the old huts. The new houses formed two parallel lines a hundred feet apart that swept down from the forest in a gentle curve for about three hundred yards. Fifty-foot palm trees had been felled and uprooted, and their trunks stripped of bark, and they had been carried back to the village with songs and shouts of triumph. There they had been re-erected down each side of the village beside the houses, and to their trunks were bound the fruits of the earth: yams and taro, sweet-potatoes and cucumbers, and marrows, and bunches of sugar cane, and bananas, and at their bases were heaped smoked pandanus nuts, and game from the forest.

At the head and foot of the village were two huge men's houses facing each other down the length of the courtyard, their great painted faces shouting silently in frozen rage. In the centre of the courtyard, to one side, was a tall platform raised about thirty feet from the ground, reached by a ladder, and from which skulls and other bones swung in net bags; it had been decorated in red, yellow, blue, and other less-definable tints until no square inch was left unadorned.

For the men of Dolivi were the hosts in a great feast, in honour of their fathers' bones, and the spirits of their ancestors. Every ten years or so, when the men of the village had accumulated enough pigs, they built a dance village and invited their neighbours to dance and display themselves before the unmarried girls, until on the final day they killed all the pigs in an orgy of slaughter.

Some guests had been living there for weeks, dancing every night and sleeping during the day, but the climax of the festival was tonight. The Dolivi women were down in the valley cutting cane for the torches to be used through the night, or helping their menfolk lure the pigs with sweet-potatoes so they could be caught and trussed for the morrow. The children ran through the forest, seeking flowers and berries with which to adorn themselves, and the old men sat in the men's houses, cracked nuts, smoked, and reminisced.

The people of Laripa came thick upon the track, and the inhabitants of Ganipa and Sapo, Niovoro and Lavalava, Mivana and Tolava, and many others, flowed over the narrow pass above Dolivi. Some paused here, in and around the government rest house that had been erected long since by Fletcher for the benefit of travellers caught by the rain, which at these altitudes could soon kill a native by exposure. Here they smoked or slept, waiting for friends in other parties to catch up with them. Whenever a Morok stopped upon the road for more than a minute or so at a time, he lit a fire, compulsively, and without necessarily seeming to enjoy it, or even to notice it. And here, too, many little fires were smoking and crackling, made of small heaps of debris collected from beneath the trees and mixed with the oily leaves of the pandanus palm to obtain a blaze. The Moroks huddled around them, smoking and chatting, squatting on their haunches, with their bundles of finery for the dance that evening by their sides.

Among them sat Fletcher, for he enjoyed nothing so much as these private walkabouts, without the encumbrance of police and carriers, when he could roam at will in his mountains, passing unseen by a sleeping hamlet in the dim radiance of early dawn, or coming in the night upon some little hut, half hidden, from which came a low murmur of voices and the occasional flurry of sparks as someone stirred the fire. There he would sit, gazing into the flames, and eating a roasted sweet-potato, listening to talk of gardens, and hunting, and the ways of pigs, until sleep overtook him. He was a familiar sight to the people as he forded the sparkling waters of a torrent, or ate a meal of fruit in the shade of some rocks by the track, or sat on the verandah of a men's house talking of nothing in particular with the chiefs. On these expeditions he made no arrests, and needed no police or bodyguard; the aura of his personality was safeguard enough for Tikame.

On this occasion, it was not only his love for the wild land which he had ruled for a decade that brought him to Dolivi, but a desire to escape from Ungabunga. It was not so much that he resented the changes there—as he'd anticipated, they were pathetic and laughable—but after two months he needed to get away to collect his thoughts, especially on the subject of police morale, which was suffering severely under the constraints of the new regime. Earlier in the day he had met Smith coming in the opposite direction, from Laripa, who gave him the news about the latrines.

"I do not think the people will listen, Roj, but I tell them. If they do nothing, who cares? The climate is good, the water is clean." He shrugged his shoulders.

"Yeah, well, you've done your job, Smithy. Get any good specimens?"

"No, Roj, very dull. Only an enlarged thyroid, a prolapsed rectum, and dental caries. I am wasting my talents here. But I must hurry, there is an autopsy at Ungabunga waiting for me. You will miss it, I think?"

"Yeah, I'll be up here a few days yet."

"Ah, a pity, and I have some excellent sherry just come special for the autopsy."

"Never mind, there'll be others."

They parted then, and Fletcher had shaken his head. Smithy was a decent bloke, all right, but he was sure as hell more than one brick short of a load.

But their meeting had been hours ago, and now the sun was well below the peaks. Already Dolivi was deep in shadow, and fires in the houses could be glimpsed from the head of the pass. Fletcher and his companions rose, suddenly cold and hungry, and began the last stage of the descent to Dolivi.

The moon had risen, though it was frequently obscured by clouds, and when the dance began, a strong wind blew down from the peaks. The coming of darkness cast a powerful spell over the village; it was no longer an ordinary space between two lines of houses, but a limitless stage whose borders were as wide as the natives' imaginations. The Beings in their great feather head-dresses who entered upon this stage were not the stunted little men of daylight, but moving idols, superhuman monsters towering to the height of the houses around them, and lit by the torches of blazing cane waved by the women who danced adoringly before them. Great clouds of smoke from these brands swept across the dance yard, blown by the strong wind, and in the fitful yellow glare, the incredible figures of the night dancers seemed to reach up to the ragged clouds.

Tossing and lashing in the dance, three hundred giants thundered upon their drums, and their song bellowed out like the notes of a mighty organ, reverberating down the gorges above the tumult of the waters and the forest, until even in distant Laripa the old men stirred among the ashes and dreamed of their youth. As the dancers stamped and pounded with tireless fury, they seemed to have taken on the qualities of the culture-heroes, the Before-Men, when time itself was not, beautiful as birds, with the endurance and virility of giants, melodiously exulting in their strength and roaring their triumphs across the ranges.

Not all their songs were of warriors and blood; some were melancholy, the infinitely sad laments of bewildered and primitive men who found themselves in a world they had not made, and could not unmake again. Fletcher, whose cigarette had long since gone out, sat on the verandah of the men's house, held in the grip of these mighty forces, staring, his eyes unfocused.

Towards one o'clock, the storm, whose flashes and rumblings had been growing steadily nearer, burst upon the village and the mountains above in all its fury. But though the dancers were scattered by the lashing rain, and awed by the searing strikes of lightning, they were not disheartened, for Nature herself had taken up and surpassed what they had begun. The ancestors were pleased.

Under the dripping eaves of the houses men struggled in the darkness with their great head-dresses, trying to remove them before the feathers were irreparably damaged by the rain. The men's houses were packed with naked bodies glistening with rain, sweat, and ornamental grease; the fires down the centres of the houses had been replenished with long dry timbers drawn from the stock beneath the floor, so that in the foetid heat and press, smelling of hot wet bodies and animal odours it was like being in the warm churnings of a great beast's innards. The wind-driven rain slatted furiously against the roofs, some of which were stripped away in a rattling hail of leaves. The men waited nervously for each gust of wind to come roaring through the streaming darkness, like a huge wave, surging through the forest, to crash upon the houses which quivered and groaned under the successive shocks.

About an hour before dawn, Fletcher awoke and crawled through the entrance to stretch himself outside and have a smoke. With the passing of the storm the night sky had gradually cleared, and when Fletcher emerged, the stars were shining and the air was scented with the rich odours of wet earth and rotting leaves. The valley was filled with white mists that lay utterly still, a scene of astonishing quietness and peace.

When the sun was risen, the people of Dolivi and their guests set about bringing the pigs into the dance yard and pegging them out for slaughter, a task which occupied the whole morning. Many were huge brutes, covered in long, black, coarse hair, and long-snouted as ant-eaters, an ancient breed that ran half-wild in the forests. The men passed long poles between their tethered legs and hoisted them onto their shoulders, shrieking and kicking in their bonds, for the short journey into the centre of the village, where they were pegged by the feet to hold them steady when the time came for them to be clubbed to death. By midday the dance-yard was filled from end to end with two rows of pigs, about five hundred beasts in all, some comatose, some with heaving flanks and restless, twisting heads, some shrieking intermittently and kicking against the stakes.

Meantime, the guests had assembled on either side of the dance-yard in expectation of the entrance of the chief of Dolivi, Marbek, and his warriors. From the forest came the distant shouts of furiously angry men that grew louder every second, and in a few moments the horde of Dolivi warriors, led by Marbek whirling his club Despair and Die, overwhelmed the stockade at the entrance of the village, uprooting and scattering the stakes, as the guests pretended to cower in fear, and ran down the carpet of pigs' bodies to stand, each man on a writhing pig, club raised, shouting the war-cry of Dolivi, with the red juice of the betel nut running down their chins.

Marbek, who was carrying a sack, was joined by Fletcher at the foot of the ladder and they both mounted slowly and with dignity to the platform. Fletcher sat on an ornamental bench while Marbek launched into an hour-long evocation of the glorious deeds of the fathers of Dolivi, with whose bones some of the guests had been dancing in string bags the previous night, a greatly coveted honour.

Marbek was a squat man with a huge hooked nose, through the septum of which a cassowary's wing-bone was thrust, and mutton-chop whiskers, a fashion started by the first Resident Magistrate in 1906. He was a man of immense self-confidence and bogus genial-ity, with a harsh, penetrating voice. His speech recalled the great days before the government, when Gaajok had led Dolivi to pillage and rape and kill from Laripa to Mivana, even to Niovoro; Gaajok, who never slept in his bed, but prowled and padded through the night, axe over his shoulder, his cold eyes piercing the darkness as he searched for living things to kill. Or Longar, who could always be counted on to contribute a note of hilarity to an afternoon's slaugh-ter by stuffing potatoes into the mouths of the dying, or cutting off their fingers and toes and putting them to cook in the ashes of the fires, with the sweet-potatoes, so that the survivors should find them when they came back to eat their evening meal, and weep again. Or Pagong, who had once pinned three children to a tree with a single thrust of his black-palm spear when he came upon them suddenly out of the smoke of their burning village. Things were quieter now, but the battles of land-dispute day, and the duels which Fletcher al-lowed for settling individual grievances, were some compensation, and had produced their modern heroes in every village, virtuosi of cudgel and shield, whose records and performances were eagerly de-bated by Morok youth.

His speech was heard in rapt silence, interrupted only once by a village cur which began yapping querulously; it was instantly silenced with a club.

Now Marbek turned to review the events of the last few months; the arrival of the Father of Nyikang; the vast quantites of cargo landed at Ungabunga; the strange new houses, and the red people who lived in them. He paid tribute to Tikame's new friends, and to their wealth, and to Tikame for bringing them to share it with the Moroks, but underlying his words was the clear hint that, while Tikame was a great man, he was a hard man, and that for the time being, at any rate, they would do well to appease these new and gentler beings who for some inexplicable reason seemed to have more power at the moment. The present trend of events was clearly unlikely to last; it was said that the old fortress and gaol were to be demolished, doubtless to make room for much bigger and stronger ones, but while there was no fear of prison and the police, men could relax for a while.

When he reached the climax of his speech he held up the sack, which clinked and rattled. Then, with a dramatic gesture, he whipped off the bag and revealed the contents—a brand-new gin trap, of a size that might have been used to capture lions. It was one of the traps sent in error to Elephant Island and now being zealously distributed by Tristram Daubeny to all the Moroks he could find at Ungabunga. This one had been brought only the other day by a prisoner just released from gaol, one of the expendable members of the Dolivi tribe, ingratiating, rat-faced, slinking and down-trodden by his kin; qualities that endeared him to Daubeny, but which ensured that his new possession was instantly wrenched from him as soon as he stepped inside his village.

"O men of Dolivi, see what the Father of Nyikang hath sent me. He hath sent it as a gift, since he well knows that I am a great man, a chief, and the son of chiefs, and the begetter of chiefs, and it is fitting that chiefs should bestow gifts upon one another. He hath sent it that I may trap meat in the forests of my ancestors, to fill my belly, and make it hot with flesh. So what beast shall we trap, I and my kin, with this gift of the Father of Nyikang? For there are many beasts in the forest, and some are too small, and some are too swift for this trap, and others are too cunning, and yet others stink. But there is one beast which our fathers used to hunt, before the red men came and forbad them, which now runs free, and roots in our gardens; it cometh in the night, and maketh sorcery against us, and it is not too small, and it is not too swift, and it is not too cunning, and its flesh is sweet. This is the beast that I shall hunt."

This elaborate allegory—elaborate partly for the pleasure of it, partly out of politeness to Fletcher, who still represented government authority—confused no one. The hunted beast was to be Man.

As Marbek finished his peroration, he flung the trap into the yard below with a clatter of iron plates and chain; it was the signal for the massacre to begin. With frenzied cries, nostrils dilated, the slaughterers leapt to assault the pigs with a hail of blows to their jaws and skulls, smashing teeth, dislodging eyeballs, and sending streams of blood from their nostrils. The spectators, maddened by the crack of clubs on skulls, the yells of the warriors, and the agonized shrieks of the pigs, lost all control over themselves, and began tearing down houses as well as the stockade to provide themselves with clubs to join in the butchery. Beating aside the village curs, which scuttled about lapping the blood trickling from the snouts of the pigs, they flung themselves on the dying animals.

One pig, less securely tied than the others, managed to break free, and made a desperate rush to escape the agony of those smashing blows, darting and twisting, half-blinded, among the legs of the slaughterers and spectators. They turned on it with axes, spears, rocks and hut posts; within ten yards a back leg was nearly severed by an axe, and as it lunged for the shaded security which lay beneath the huts, a barbed black-palm spear ripped into its belly. It stopped, then wrenched itself free, spilling out yards of pearly-purple intestines from the gash, that trailed behind it in the mud.

At Ungabunga, Prout and his colleagues had taken advantage of Fletcher's absence to accomplish the destruction of the fort and gaol. An invitation had been sent to the three nearest villages to come and destroy the hated instruments of their oppression, and now like ants around the carcass of some fat insect, they were scurrying to and fro with the spoils. While they didn't have the slightest idea why Prout had invited them to destroy the fort, they were not slow to take advantage of a free load of well-seasoned timber and corrugated iron.

Prout and his wife watched, with benign satisfaction, the success of this first attempt at political education.

"I think it's wonderful what you've accomplished in so short a time, dear," said Phyllis. "All the departments set up, the suppression of Fletcher and the police, and now this. You're really a very remarkable man, do you know that?"

He squeezed her arm tenderly.

"No, dear, I really mean it."

"Well, we mustn't get complacent. There's a tremendous amount still to be done. This is just damping down the smouldering ashes in the ruins, disinfecting the bomb site. Now we must build. Clean, and fresh, and new."

They stood in silence for a while, watching a group of Moroks heaving on the timbers of the gatehouse in the stockade. Suddenly it collapsed on them, knocking several to the ground.

"Gracious, I hope no one's hurt," said Phyllis.

"I don't think so. Thank heavens, they're a tough people."

"I should think they need to be, after all they've been through from Fletcher. I wonder what they were like before the white man came?"

"Very hard to say, dear. But obviously white rule has brought out the worst in them. When you have sadists like Fletcher encouraging them to fight, and denying them basic amenities, can you wonder that they do behave rather violently at times?"

"Of course. Do you think that in their original state they would have fought at all?"

"Humankind is naturally peaceful," said Prout, with a didactic glaze coming over his eyes. "The main causes of war have been kings, who drove their subjects into battle for their own ambitions, and priestly superstition, such as the Crusades, but clearly there were no kings or priests here. While, as I have always maintained, the environmental stress and lack of protein would have stimulated some degree of violence, we realised at Manchester that all conflict in simple societies tends to resolve itself pretty quickly, due to something called "cross-cutting ties." So of course there would always have been quarrelling, and some violence now and then, but a state of equilibrium would have been reached before it could go very far. Imperialism has been the basic cause of warfare in societies like this, of which Fletcher's regime was a textbook case. And when you think of the appalling violence we Europeans have inflicted on each other, let alone on the colonial peoples, I should say that, relatively speaking, these were really very peaceful people, by nature."

"So it is the white man's presence here that has disturbed the natural balance of the society, and led to so much violence today?"

"Oh yes, we've got a lot to answer for."

The pigs had been gutted with axes at Dolivi, and the innards cut out for transportation by the women. The men who were dismembering the carcases were bloody to their elbows, very nearly as bloody as their long-handled axes.

As soon as the pigs had been distributed, and the pork made ready for the guests' departures, the last act of the drama commenced. Malek from Laripa, Abuk of Lavalava, Deng of Niovoro, and Matiang of Mivana stepped forward ceremonially to abuse their hosts with the most obscene insults their imaginations could suggest. Taking their bows, they began firing arrows into the principal men's house while they expressed their utter contempt for their hosts; for their grudging hospitality, their stringy pork, their smelly women, and their tiny penises. They were backed enthusiastically in this by their men, and the warriors of Dolivi withdrew, growling and menacing their guests with spears, until they had formed up outside the village at the edge of the forest. The women of the guests had been making a rapid exit during these proceedings, scurrying off with their pork to a safe distance before matters became serious.

Once the women of both sides were safely away, the guests began in earnest. Singing derisive songs, they dashed hither and thither with burning brands, hurling them into the two men's houses, and thrusting them under the leaves of every hut. In a few minutes, dense smoke and crackling flames burst from the houses, as the fresh oily leaves were sucked up by the leaping flames. The great platform was torn down in a chaos of splintering wreckage, while other men, yelling like fiends, were uprooting the great trees, still thickly festooned with vegetables on their upper parts, and heaving them over so that they crashed into the blazing dwellings, sending up great spouts of smoke and sparks. When the village was well alight and truly devastated, the guests fled as if for their lives, because the men of Dolivi were descending on them from the forest with cries of fury that were almost genuine. As the guests legged it for the river, and the safety of the other bank, they were sped on their way by showers of arrows. One guest, a little too enthusiastic about his ceremonial duties, halted on a rock above the ford, and, bending down, began slapping his buttocks in contempt at the pursuing enemy. As might be expected, he got a swift arrow up the rump for his pains and skipped through the shallows hopping and yelling for help from his mates, who were safely in the shelter of the trees.

Fletcher, who had left before the firing of the village, regarded the scene with satisfaction. Dance villages were filthy places after these affairs, and burning them was the best thing to be done. As he rode towards Laripa, threading his way among the files of guests, he brooded on the rumours of destruction at Ungabunga.

Chapter VIII

ARM PIT CREEK was a small tributary of the Loma River, and the site of Ned Oakley's mining camp, where he and a few Moroks spent their days shovelling wash dirt into the sluice boxes, removing and cleaning the riffles, panning the residues, and regulating the water flow from the dam. It was an old-fashioned method, but Oakley was in no hurry. The claim was not only unusually rich, but was also the last payable one left on the island, as far as he knew, and he knew every creek, having prospected for several years before lighting on Arm Pit Creek, or Amipiti, as the natives called it. The white quartz and brown ironstone rocks had been more than a nod to a blind horse, and the colors of his first dish had told him that his fortune was made.

Having found his gold, the next problem was to keep it. Digging it out of the ground was just a matter of hiring a dozen or so native boys. The Elephant Island administration had always been short of cash, and the mirage of gold, another Edie Creek or a Yodda, had bewitched the brains of distant administrators in Queensland, Port Moresby and Rabaul, as they shuffled the responsibility for the remote and useless island between each other. The coastal population being too small, and the swamps too extensive to make copra an economic proposition, gold or perhaps osmiridium looked the only chance of lightening the financial burden of what Sir Hubert Murray in one of his despatches from Papua had once referred to as "one of our more tiresome dependencies, whose pacification is likely to be as fruitless for its inhabitants as it will be costly for us."

To make sure that the revenues from the vital, if elusive, gold should not slip through the palsied fingers of bureaucracy by some legal fumbling, it was early decided to make the Warden of the Goldfields a direct appointment of the King-in-Council, with the responsibility of imposing a 20 percent tax on all gold removed from the island that would be used solely to defray governmental costs. The Resident Magistrate was merely appointed by whichever Administration had been pressed by the other two into doing so. Their foresight had been amply rewarded between the wars, when a number of strikes had been made that covered the costs of administering the island a hundred times over.

But tax was the least of Oakley's worries. If news of the strike leaked out, the place would be flooded with diggers and worked to the bone in a year. So he needed a Warden who understood his problems and could be relied on to bring a fresh and unprejudiced mind to their solution. For fifteen per cent each, Fletcher and Oelrichs had agreed to suppress all news of the strike and officially represented Oakley's output as a few ounces a month, as that was the minimum amount necessary to keep together the body and soul of a slightly crazy digger, and act as bait to keep him hooked to his claim, but not enough to attract the notice of prospectors anywhere else in Australia or the South Pacific. Fletcher issued Oakley's yearly Miner's Right, for the sum of two pounds seventeen shillings and sixpence, payable within thirty days of the expiry of the last Right, and registered his claims as they were pegged. Since the total value of the gold so far extracted was in excess of seven hundred thousand pounds sterling, his clerical labours were rather well rewarded.

The camp was a simple affair comprising tool shed, store, boy-house, kitchen and wash-house, and Oakley's cabin. A rope was slung between this and the wash-house, on which an assortment of woollen underwear, tartan shirts, and denim trousers swung gently in the light airs, scattering a shower of drops on the dry, shiny stones beneath. Palio, Oakley's cooky, returned to the stove after hanging the washing out and began to brew afternoon tea. He was a grizzled Manus Islander, who had carried for Shark Eye Park on the Edie as a lad, and had remained with a series of diggers as sluicer, boss-boy, general factotum, and cooky ever since. He knew only two basic dishes, "stiu," which was a mess of baked beans and bully-beef, heated and beaten together, and "carri," which was the same, but with some curry powder added. Luckily for him, Oakley was not a gourmet.

Oakley's cabin was a one-room leaf shack, with a verandah and a shutter in the side that could be propped open to let in light and air, and closed against the weather. In the room was a hammock, with some rather skungy blankets, slung along the wall opposite the window, and above it was a crucifix. Opposite the door was a stack of shelves filled with an assortment of books, including Capablanca's "My Hundred Best Games," Newman's "Apologia," a set of Dickens, and Sopwith's "Assay Techniques for Precious Metals"; tobacco tins of assorted greasy nuts and bolts, and occasionally tobacco; torch batteries, cartridges, and some socks of dubious cleanliness.

In the centre of the room was a table of native manufacture, with a couple of rough chairs, over which a Coleman lamp hung on a hook from a beam. The space under the floor was filled with stacks of bully-beef tins bound with wire and old rum bottles, all packed with gold-dust.

Oakley had gone up to the dam with one of his boys for some target practice; he was a crack shot with a .303, and as a young man had won a crate of Ned Kelly off Arthur Darling, though to be fair Arthur was in failing health by then. He had recently replenished his supply of targets by having his boys raid the Mission's stores at Ungabunga, on his last visit. They had collected, among other things, most of the ceramic ash-trays, which the boy was now engaged in tossing into the air from behind a rock, to be shattered by Oakley perched thirty yards away in a tree. What age had taken from his skill, experience had restored, and he was, if anything, a rather better shot than in the days of his youth in Papua when he had driven O'Regan the Rager, Bluey Arvold, and Alligator Jack Stinson off his claim on the Yodda, snivelling with funk, with what the Assistant Resident Magistrate had described in his report as "perhaps the most remarkable display of musketry with the Martini-Enfield that I have ever seen."

Fletcher tethered his horse to the rail outside the camp and, hearing the shooting, went and flung himself in a deck-chair on the verandah, calling for some tea. Oakley arrived shortly after the tea and sat down in the other chair, propping his rifle against the wall of the shack, and pouring himself a mug of the steaming brew.

"I've been hearin' things about the station on me trip. The orlies been tearin' it apart, have they?" asked Fletcher.

"That's about the strength of it. The kanakas runnin' like Sydneysiders to a fire in a brewery, and Prout and his missus beamin' and lordin' it over the whole proceedings, like two plaster saints, expectin' the Good Lord to come down from Heaven and pat 'em on the head."

"A boot up the arse, more like," rasped Fletcher. "I'll 'ave to be away first thing tomorrer mornin', Ned. Go down and get among 'em. Can't let 'em get away with this."

"Well, take it easy, mate. We've got another year before the best of this claim's worked out, and the price of gold being what it is we can't afford to lose it by you getting slung out."

"Yer'll be OK, Ned. Nobody'll bother yer. But this is personal between me and Prout and those other rat bags."

After supper on the verandah, which was curtained with mosquito netting to keep off the beetles, they played chess in the glare of the Coleman, and sipped their coffee and rum. Apart from gold, chess was the principal obsession of Oakley's waking hours, and no visitor was allowed to leave without playing at least a half-dozen games.

"There's a letter there for Father Jules," said Oakley, while Fletcher was pondering the implications of a double rook attack. "Don't forget it. I've done for 'im good and proper this time. He'll have to resign. Loses his bishop, too—hopeless position!" He was referring to the latest move in the game of postal chess which he was conducting with Father Jules Duroc, a priest in Papua, "a real missionary," as he always referred to the man.

"Yeah, I won't forget. How long since you and him been playing?"

"I dunno. Met him before the war, near the Yodda. Livin' rougher than me, teaching the kanakas to grow coffee and such like. Knows the language, and takes no bloody nonsense from 'em neither. Number one bloke. Somethin' of a saint to my way o' thinkin'. It's your move, y' know. 'Ave some more rum."

Fletcher, to his own surprise, succeeded in pulling the game out of the fire by some adroit pawn play in the final moves, and Oakley upended the dregs of the bottle into his mug. As he rummaged for a fresh one, he said:

"Why not call it quits, Roj? Prout and his mob'll win in the end. You can't turn back the clock. With your cut down there," he tapped his carpet slipper on the boards indicating the gold beneath, "you've got it made for life. Those bastards aren't worth breakin' your neck for."

"Yer dead right there, Ned. Truth is, though, I'm part of this place now. Forgotten what Australia's like, and don't want to know, either. And say what yer like, these blokes may be a murderin' bunch of bastards, but they've got somethin' about 'em the white man's lost."

"They've got something all right—pure bloody evil! I don't mind tellin' yer, this place gives me the creeps sometimes."

"Ah, come off it, Ned, they're bad buggers all right, but the way yer talk yer make it sound like Old Nick 'imself was sittin' up in the mountains. I still say these blokes 'ave more goin' for 'em in the way o' guts and life than those whingein' little runts mowin' their lawns in the suburbs."

There was a long silence, filled by the steady hiss of the Coleman lamp. Oakley replenished their glasses, and set up the board for their next game.

"Best o' five, then Roj? You won the last, so it's your move."

The next morning Fletcher was on the road at dawn, leaving Oakley to his breakfast of tea and porridge and chewing tobacco. In less than two hours he had reached Ungabunga, where he galloped up the centre of the strip, clods flying, just to show he was back. At the top of the strip, by the aircraft apron, was a knot of strangers, pasty-faced narrow-shouldered clerks in white shorts and Aertex shirts, and neat stockings, with their nondescript wives, three of whom were heavily pregnant. A number of snotty-nosed infants were crawling and tottering in the middle of the strip, shrieking petulantly for attention. Fletcher thundered through them and reined up Monckton, his bay stallion, just in front of the group of parents. They had watched his cavalier progress up the strip with increasing resentment, and his traumatic horsemanship in the presence of their offspring moved them to indignation.

"Speak to him, Cyril," said a dumpy, waspish blonde, "You are Senior Clerk, you know."

"Hey, mate," said Cyril, a sandy haired, gangling fellow, with a prominent Adam's apple, "You ought to watch where you're going. There are kiddies playing down there, you know."

Murmurs of agreement supported this rebuke.

Fletcher turned a reflective stare upon him and the rest of the group. Before leaving Arm Pit Creek he had borrowed a quid of Oakley's tobacco for the journey, and there was now a rich, dark infusion of nicotine broth swirling between his teeth. After letting his eyes rest on them for a few moments longer he projected it in a powerful stream onto the ground in front of them. Public defecation could not have shocked them more. They drew back in revulsion, with mutterings of "ah, dirty bastard... who *is* that bloke, anyway?" and scattered as he trotted Monckton silently through them and rode back to his residence.

There he found Moncreif still in bed, with three of Fletcher's "wives," stark naked, feeding him thin slices of buttered toast and sips of gin. Fletcher despatched his womenfolk, giggling, with slaps on their rumps.

"They never ruddy well give me drinks in bed. Didn't know they could make toast, neither."

"You don't deserve them, old chap. Splendid girls, only need a bit of breaking in to civilized ways. I was showing them a few little tricks, actually, that even Masters and Johnson have never heard of, and they took to them like ducks to water."

"Masters and Johnson, eh? Sound like a coupl'a perves to me. That's the trouble with yer Poms. Never like it plain and simple. Anyway, while yer've been corruptin' me women, bloody Prout and the loonies've done this place over good and proper. Fort gone, orderly room gone, gaol gone, Jeez, we're lucky they even left the pub."

"Well, I *have* heard dark rumours that it's to be converted into a sewing circle for Morok ladies."

"Fair's fair, Mike, but while ye've been exercisin' the ferret, we've all landed up shit creek."

"Yes. I suppose that's true. Still, give me a few minutes to get dressed, and I shall bring my mighty intellect to bear on your problems."

"I'm goin' over to Olly's. Come over yerself when yer ready."

A while later they were sitting in Oelrich's residence, where the master of the establishment gave them the latest news. They sat for some time in gloomy silence.

"There was nothing I could do. They treat me as a figure of fun," said Oelrichs. "It was like watching some evil-minded children playing with matches and being a poor old aunty just flapping about the place being completely ignored."

"Well, Mike, you're the legal genius. Where do I stand as RM? Can they get away with this?"

"Yes, unfortunately they can. Of course, they should have consulted you first, but Canberra has placed your position, and its powers, at the discretion of the Special Commissioner until the new constitution is ratified and independence is granted, in a year or so. There's nothing to stop him making the first native he sees the RM if he wants to."

"But they've never made up their minds if this place is run from Moresby, Rabaul, or Canberra. That's how we got away with this for so long."

"Makes no difference now. When the chips are down, Canberra has the last word. All appointments are made by Canberra, and they can unmake them."

"There is one appointment to the establishment of this station that is not made by Canberra," said Oelrichs, looking up at the ceiling.

"Yeah, a padre. Last one we had here croaked in '43, never been replaced."

"I was thinking of the Warden of the Goldfields."

"God Almighty, yer right."

"But there aren't any goldfields here," said Moncreif.

"Oh yes, there flamin' well are, and I'm the Warden. I've got Letters Patent to prove it. From the Queen-in-Council."

"Do you have the papers?" asked Moncreif.

Oelrichs rose from his chaise longue and went over to a Regency escritoire, from which, after some fumbling, he produced the Letters Patent and handed them to Moncreif.

"Anyhow, what difference does it make, Olly? Prout'll tell me to stuff the goldfields."

After some minutes' silence, while he examined the documents, Moncreif pronounced his verdict.

"It seems to be what we've been looking for. It's a very powerful position, in fact. They were obviously determined that the revenues should be secured at all costs, whatever else they might argue about. Your post as Comptroller of Excises comes with the Wardenship, incidentally. You're entitled to inspect all imported goods, and levy such duties as from time to time you deem expedient, not to exceed 20 percent of their gross retail value; to issue Miners' Rights and Leases, register claims, supervise assaying, and recruit a police force to maintain order on the goldfields if necessary."

He looked up from the document with a broad grin. "A police force! You realise what that means? It looks as if you're back in business again. It'll take at least a year for Prout to petition the Privy Council to dismiss you, and for all the formalities to be completed.

By which time, if your luck holds, he'll be out on his ear anyway after making a first class balls-up of this place."

"Bloody marvellous," said Fletcher. "Shows yer what brains can do, don't it, Olly?"

"It does indeed, dear boy."

"So Fletcher's Irregulars can ride again?"

"I don't see why not. You should change their title to "Goldfields Constabulary," or something like that, but once they're officially constituted by you, in a proclamation to that effect, Prout won't be able to touch you. Of course, your powers will be restricted to offences related to law and order on the goldfields, that's the only problem."

"Yeah, but the orlies won't know that, and once we're off the station Prout won't know what we do!"

"There might be a lot to be said for not using the police too vigorously, for the time being," said Oelrichs. "Give Prout enough rope to hang himself, let things go to pot."

"I see what yer mean. We don't want to do their work for 'em. They reckon they can do without the police, so let 'em. But I'll have to lick 'em back into shape again. We'll have a parade this afternoon. Mounted drill, the lot. Sweat the booze out of 'em. Might even go and collect some customs duties. Talkin' of customs duties, what's that dozy lot o' bastards doin' here, the ones wanderin' all over the strip when I came in?"

"Oh, they're the new clerks, a dozen of them, and their families. Came in on Monday," said Oelrichs. "There'll be more later, apparently."

"Yeah, I reckoned they were shiny-arses when I said "G'day" to 'em." He described his encounter with relish.

"You were terribly beastly to them. They're only poor little chickens, really, absolutely harmless," said Moncreif.

"Chooks! Too bloody right, they're chooks! Whingin', runty little bastards. Should've stayed back in the big smoke where they belong. 'Fore long the place'll be crawlin' with 'em. Anyhow, we'll be through 'em like a dose o' salts this afternoon. Go and search 'em for contraband. If I find any dirty books I'll bring 'em over."

Fletcher went off roaring for the sergeant-major to give him the good news. The men were similarly enlightened after being kicked out of the whore-house by the NCOs and suffering a lightning kit inspection by the sergeant-major during which all but one man, in the sick bay, were put on jankers for idle belts, idle buttons, idle haircuts and every other form of idleness that the frustrated imagination of the sergeant-major could conjure up. As the familiar routine clamped round them once more, their eyes regained their wonted brightness, their backs straightened, and their idle petulance was smoothed away.

The afternoon repose of the residents of Ungabunga was broken by the shouts of command of Fletcher and the sergeant-major, as they dressed, open-ordered, advanced, wheeled, and charged their troop up and down the strip. For this occasion, ceremonial lances had been issued, to boost morale, and groups of Europeans drifted out to the edge of the strip to watch the display.

Fletcher formed up his men in line, and after an impressive performance by the buglers, he officially informed them that they were now the Royal Mounted Goldfields Constabulary, answerable only to him, and beyond the reach of any white man. He gave them a short smoko to digest the new situation, and informally answered their questions. During this lull, Treadwell was seen making a portentious approach. Even more purple than usual, he strode energetically across the grass and seized Fletcher's bridle.

"What the bloody 'ell do you think you're doing, Fletcher, disturbing folks on a Saturday afternoon?"

"What's it look like, Obadiah?" Fletcher, who had discovered Treadwell's secret, lingered over the hated middle name with a sneer.

Treadwell cringed, and said, in a slightly more conciliatory tone, "it looks as if you're disobeying Dr Prout, Fletcher. You know all militaristic parades and such-like are strictly forbidden. This is flagrant contempt for United Nations' authority."

"Well, for yer information, Obadiah, I'm exercisin' my legal rights, under Royal Letters Patent, as Warden of the Goldfields, to establish a new police force." He extended his hand in the direction of his men. "So yer can take yer United Nations' authority and stick it up Prout's nose."

"Do you know who you are addressing?"

"Who?"

"The General Secretary of the Elephant Island Trades Union Committee."

'Yeah? Well go and call a General Strike, then, if it'll make yer feel better. Ye're lookin' a bit crook, tell yer the truth, mate. Too much twangin' the wire, most like."

Almost epileptic with rage at this final assault on his dignity, Treadwell made a grab at Fletcher's leg in an attempt to unseat him. Monckton wheeled sharply, throwing Treadwell to the ground, to hoots and shrieks of laughter from the police. Ponderously, swearing hideous oaths peculiar to the brotherhood of gas-fitters, he struggled to his feet and withdrew from the field, falling into the drainage ditch as he turned to give Fletcher a final piece of his mind.

In high spirits after this interlude, the new Constabulary turned their attention to rousting out the store-sheds and houses of the Mission personnel, in a vigorous search for contraband. Since nothing brought in by the staff had been declared for Customs purposes, Fletcher considered he had a free hand; the general rubric under which the search was conducted defined "contraband" as anything

CHAPTER VIII 97

that might entertain his men, or whose disclosure might embarrass its owners.

"Must get Mike to tidy up the Ordinance on Customs and Excise," said Fletcher to himself, as he drove a boot into the glossy white sliding doors of a kitchen cupboard, splintering them and smashing most of the crockery behind them. He was in Cyril's house, and Cyril was presently cowering in the living room with his wife as the Warden and his men provided them with a fair imitation of the Assyrian army in one of its more Biblical moods. The crash of glass and china as Sgt Oala tore down some shelves in the house next door reassured him of the diligence of the search.

Trooper Gumbo disinterred some *Playboy* magazines from under a record-player, and a group of his mates gathered round him, open-mouthed. Attracted by their sniggering, Fletcher came back to the living room. He rounded on Cyril.

"Call yerself an Australian? Ya dirty perve. Readin' rotten shit'ouse stuff like this in front of yer missus."

Cyril looked as if he intended to object to this analysis of his character.

"And none of yer bloody lip, neither, or I'll flamin' flatten yer." Kicking the legs off a sideboard, to emphasise the moral rigour of his position, he led his men out of the house with their booty.

As dusk fell, having given the chooks and the rest of the Mission a day to remember, with the sole exception of the Prouts, who were away, the Royal Mounted Goldfields Constabulary dispersed to quarters, equipped with large quantities of confiscated booze, playing cards, cigarettes, and dirty picture books.

Chapter IX

WHEN THE PROUTS returned from their trip to Port Moresby, they were aghast at the fury of Fletcher's reprisals. And when they saw his wanton destruction in the Mission houses, and heard of the brutal humiliations of the staff, Prout's previous contempt was transformed into a vivid personal hatred.

His immediate reaction was to send a note to Fletcher, giving him a week to make arrangements to leave the island, but the day after sending it, Moncreif casually informed him of Fletcher's legal impregnability. In a mood of baffled rage, he dismissed Fletcher from his post as Resident Magistrate, and all associated offices, and began the tedious proceedings to petition the Privy Council to also deprive Fletcher of his Wardenship of the Goldfields. It was also necessary to restore the morale of his staff, which had been notably depressed by the apparent impotence of the Mission to quell the irrepressible Fletcher.

"Whatever he thinks he can do with his private army of thugs, I want to reassure you that the days of police rule and gaols have gone for good," he told his staff. "We won a notable victory last Saturday, in fact, by showing to all persons of good will that the true basis of his violent repression is not the welfare of the people, but his own self-interest." It was apparent even to Prout that most of his listeners considered this to be a rather thin and unsatisfying sort of victory, so he decided that he should further inspire them by visions of future progress.

"We shall consolidate our moral position by sweeping hygienic, cultural, legal and technological reforms, of which the keystone will be independence in the middle of next year. So-called practical people would criticise us for granting independence so soon, but of course, they overlook the fact that all our reforms are hampered at present by our colonialist relationship with the people. We may talk of equality between ourselves and the indigenes, and I am sure that all of us in this room sincerely believe that they *are* our equals in everything that matters, but until their land is restored to them a dark shadow will be cast over all true co-operation between us. Independence will not mean the end of our mission here but, on the contrary, will lay the foundations for a new and deeper relationship between us and the people."

This time he was warmly applauded. He also went on to explain that, since Fletcher obviously had every intention of staying on, there was no longer any need for secrecy in obtaining evidence about his murders. It was therefore with distinctly unacademic relish that Prout announced a reward for information on Fletcher's crimes was to be circulated among the people.

But the major event of the moment was the arrival of the equipment for the gas works, and its installation on the site of the old fort. The tanks and ancillary apparatus were flown in during the course of a single week, and assembled by expatriates before the end of the month, much to the wonder of the Moroks, who came in their hundreds to gaze in silence at the towering orange cylinders, and "to the lasting credit of Mr. Treadwell," as Prout expressed it during the unveiling ceremony. Miss Ursula Fratchett arrived from Melbourne to supervise the organization of the Mission library, with her staff of four, and Miss Gudrun Holmstrom finally made her appearance at the Sex Education Clinic, to begin preparing her travelling exhibition of "The Twentieth Century Orgasm."

Tristram Daubeny, the most painstaking and agitated of all the various benefactors of the Moroks, was also occupied. As a young boy he had been distinguished by an almost morbid preoccupation with the sufferings of others, for which, in a vague way, he felt personally to blame, constantly thrusting nutritious scraps upon those whom he conceived to be the deserving poor. Unfortunately, they usually turned out to be tramps or gypsies, who, after examining the eagerly proffered dainties, hurled them away with an oath when his back was turned. His other preoccupation was with "potties" and "big jobs," a propensity of mind which moved his nanny, Mrs Cumberland, to observe on more than one occasion, "you're a dirty-minded little boy, Master Tristram, and dirty-minded little boys go to an early grave."

At his public school, where there was a notable deficiency of tramps and gypsies, he deadened the pangs of guilt by owning up to the offences of others, not so much for the benefit of the culprits, but to experience the satisfaction of the punishment. On leaving school, he felt that he had already been given more than his share of this world's privileges, and earned none of them, and that to proceed to university would be, for him, an act of reprehensible greed and selfishness. A stray copy of *National Geographic* in his Housemaster's study had persuaded him, in a flash of insight, that his true vocation was to teach the uses of manure to the poor natives of Africa and Asia. The smellier the manure, the nastier the climate, and the surlier the natives, the more he relished the prospect in his fantasies. His parents were naturally grieved that his expensive education should qualify him for nothing more than "teaching wogs to shovel shit," as his father insensitively put it, but he was not to be dissuaded, and after courses at an agricultural college, and with UNESCO in Paris, he was assigned to Elephant Island.

The Moroks carried off all the traps he could provide for them, and this initial success had raised his stock considerably among his colleagues. He proposed to follow this achievement with a lecture tour through the mountains on his favorite topic, manure. All Prout's staff had been studying Pidgin English intensively, so that, by means of a few Morok interpreters, the worst communications problems had been solved. And the Moroks were looking forward to seeing Daubeny again, since they regarded him as the red man who had done most to enhance the quality of their lives.

The dam restraining the bloodlust of the Moroks had been severely weakened by the abolition of police patrols, and now the gift of the gin traps produced the first visible cracks in its walls. Memories of pig stealing, ravaging of gardens, rapes, insults, and humiliations by their neighbours crowded thick within their narrow and inflamed imaginations, and the now unparalleled opportunities for carnage provided by the current situation set them thirsting for vengeance. Soon, along the forest tracks and the paths through the high kunai grass, pattered the mountain men, their eyes glittering with feverish anticipation as they carried their new traps bound in jungle vines. Each village chose its favorite points of ambush and set up the traps, hidden by rotting logs and drifts of leaves, upon some path which was frequented by their enemies—and to the Moroks, every stranger was an enemy.

Marbek and his kin secured the first victim, a careless youth of Tolava, over the ridge from Dolivi, who came to hunt the cassowary in the forests. As he lay beside the trap, groaning and twisting, his right leg mangled by the jaws, they came and disemboweled him with a jagged branch. Other victims, more desperate, succeeded in prising open the metal jaws, and dragged their broken bodies away along the forest floor, clawing up the earth, their hearts pounding and their necks rigid with terror as they sought safety with bulging, frightened eyes. This was the best sport of all to their enemies, who enjoyed watching a victim crawl to safety, only to surround him on the brink of freedom and see his hope die, before despatching him with pitiless abandon.

The women heated stones for the earth ovens, and laid out carpets of *kovelapa* leaves, upon which the corpses were to be dismembered, for the Moroks strongly disliked eating dirty meat. The smoke of the ovens rose in all the land of the Moroks, and the songs of the hunters, their dripping prey slung on poles, filled the valleys. And under the moon the dancers thundered on their drums, their bellies hot with human flesh, and waved the bones of their enemies.

Oblivious to all this unpleasantness, Daubeny and two chooks arrived in Laripa one afternoon, exhausted but cheerful. It was now well into the rainy season, and the second half of their journey had been made in the pouring rain. But though the weeping mists hung low over Laripa, they received a tumultuous welcome. Malek, Macardit and Garang led the people, who danced out to greet them. Once installed in the rest house, a large pig was brought and killed; great quantities of yams, sweet-potatoes and smoked pandanus nuts were piled before them, and lengthy orations were delivered by Malek and the other chiefs. At length, secure in the affections of the people, they slept well.

The next morning, before delivering his lecture on the place of fertiliser in modern agriculture, Daubeny made a tour of the village and gardens. In the course of this he noticed a line of men and boys standing outside a rather imposing structure, decorated with polished bully-beef tins, beer bottles, plastic bags and other fragments of gaily-colored industrial waste.

An hour's frustrating enquiry through the interpreter and the chiefs finally dispelled the mystery. When Dr. Smith had last visited them he had expressed Prout's wish that the people should build latrines. The people had been extremely puzzled by this eccentric idea. They knew, of course, that the red men, including Tikame and Oburabu, stored their wastes at Ungabunga in stone boxes under the earth, but the Moroks had long since decided that since the red men were not human beings the ordinary rules did not apply to them. The Moroks, the True Men, had no need of such strange devices, of course, since the pigs and dogs did all the scavenging necessary, even if they were a bit slow. But it could do no harm to humour the whims of the Father of Nyikang, so they erected a ceremonial latrine in his honour. Naturally, it was only to be used when the red men came on an official visit, so as not to spoil it, and was tied up with vines the rest of the time to stop inquisitive pigs and children falling down the hole. The line of men using it were thus paying a delicate compliment to the visitors, and they expressed the hope that Daubeny liked the decorations as well.

Indeed, before the explanations had been concluded, Daubeny was besieged by the members of the latrine party asking for sticks of tobacco and newspaper as compensation for their trouble. They were the insignificant members of the village, the rubbish-men, who had been conscripted for the job by Malek the previous night, with the assurance that they would be well-rewarded by the red men. The chiefs, of course, did not intend lowering their dignity by participating in such grotesque and indecent behaviour.

Feeling obliged to humour them, Daubeny distributed the tobacco to clamorous hands, and asked for the people to be called together to hear his lecture. They responded obediently and cheerfully, as they always did when a chief from another village paid a formal visit and speeches were to be made. On this occasion they were also hoping for a handout of money, and preferably, more tobacco. The women and small children formed themselves into little groups in the background, while the men sat in a more coherent phalanx at the front. A few of the oldest men, their heads bound up in bark cloth to hide the shame of their bald heads, tottered about leaning on their sticks and cadging tobacco from the younger men.

The lecture went well enough at first. Daubeny patiently explained that the "pekpek house belong Doctor Prout" was intended to be used by all, by men and women, young and old, every day, and several times a day if possible. He informed them that Dr. Prout wanted many of these admirable houses to be built, legions of them, covering the length and breadth of Elephant Island, and that only when this was done would Dr. Prout be pleased with his children. Having explained the benefits of sanitation he passed on to the real subject of his discourse: manure.

At this stage in the Moroks' education, Daubeny thought it wise to avoid overloading their comprehension, and he planned to take them at a gentle pace through the basic principles of erosion and soil degradation, crop-rotation, and composting. Since Pidgin is not well suited to the expression of technological concepts, and the interpreter was not very competent, the lecture collapsed into a stumbling embarrassment to all concerned, especially the audience. Etiquette forbade them to get up and leave, so they sat there and stoically endured, as Daubeny argued with the interpreter, who would launch into brief, hectoring admonitions on the backwardness of bush-kanaka gardens before stopping short and requesting clarification of a point from Daubeny in long intervals of muttering collusion.

Before the first hour was up, many of the audience were dozing, and the children had long since abandoned their mothers and scampered off to play. Daubeny felt more depressed than at any time since coming to Elephant Island. These people had asked him for bread and he had given them stones. But how could he break through to them, convey to them in a few simple words and gestures the revolutionary implications for their future, and their children's future? If only there were some ecological liturgy, some universal symbolism that could burst the chains of language and brand some meaningful image upon their simple minds. Surveying his audience, dozing, scratching, talking in low murmurs, picking their noses, and utterly indifferent, his desperation overwhelmed him, and he cast feverishly about for the means of finding some definitive symbolic act with which to set their minds and hearts on fire.

Suddenly, in a moment of inspiration, he spotted an unsavoury offering that had been deposited on the grass that morning, strode forward and plunged his hands into it. He held it up as though he were Prometheus when he had introduced Man to fire. A collective shudder ran through the assembled Moroks; the sleepers awoke as at the crack of doom; idle chatterers stopped in mid-sentence, their jaws dropping; even the little children in their play faltered and stood still, gazing mutely at the astonishing spectacle before them. Under their riveted gaze he spoke in a voice of thunder.

"This fellow pekpek, you bury him along garden, by and by him make big cargo."

He flung it down, and returned their gaze defiantly. As soon as they had recovered their wits, the women fled with their babies, fearing they knew not what nameless horrors. The men leapt to their feet and broke into groups, shouting and arguing fiercely, darting significant glances in Daubeny's direction. Feeling that the lesson had got out of hand, he judged it prudent to withdraw to the rest-house and await the results.

Among the Moroks, to even bring a foot into accidental contact with excreta, of any kind, would call forth ribald insults from those who witnessed the defilement, and the resentment of the insults in turn sometimes led to violence. For a red man to do what Daubeny had just done, not secretly, or by accident, but ceremonially, in full view of hundreds, was a devastating blow to the nature of things as the Moroks knew them. Garang, as the interpreter of the strange ways of the red men, was called upon to lead the discussion.

"'Tis sorcery, lads, 'tis sorcery," he declared, "or else the spirit Bolgump hath seized him." Bolgump, one of the less malignant Morok hobgoblins, was notorious for his lavatorial humour.

After an initial discussion, they adjourned to the men's house to further debate the significance of this astonishing turn of events. Garang could produce no convincing explanation of Daubeny's behaviour beyond the fact, obvious to all, that it had some hidden meaning. They decided to be cautious and to propitiate Daubeny, who had, after all, provided them with the excellent traps, so vastly superior to their own.

As it happened, only the other day they had caught a woman of Dolivi in one of Daubeny's traps, down by the river bank where she had gone to catch frogs. After listening to her cries for an hour or so, Apuk and Macardit, whose hunting territory it was, had gone down and after enjoying a lengthy rape, they butchered her. They removed the thigh-bones, to allow the legs to be folded up neatly, and cut out the viscera, some of which they ate on the spot, and brought the rest of the meat back to Laripa. Apuk had selfishly and impolitely absconded with the head before the formal distribution, since it was a delicacy to which he was particularly partial, but not all the best bits had been consumed. Part of a breast and a hand were still left and it was proposed to make a present of these to Daubeny, to express their appreciation of the traps, and to ensure that he did not take amiss the commotion at his lecture.

But Pariak and Malek objected that, as a red man, he would not appreciate these delicacies which would be wasted on him, and that he would be quite happy with a bit of rump. Fortunately, a rubbish-man called Aiwell had put a nice piece of rump on one side in the men's house and this was appropriated, his whining objections being silenced by a scowl from Malek.

Daubeny spent that afternoon with the two clerks in a state of nervous anticipation. The interpreter fled when Daubeny made his dramatic gesture, so the three had no means of guessing what the men of Laripa would do next. It was therefore an immense relief when they saw a deputation of notables approaching the rest house at sunset bearing a parcel of leaves tied up with vine. Assembling at the foot of the steps leading up to the verandah, Malek solemnly presented the bundle while the others, smiling made claws of their fingers to simulate the action of a trap. They pointed to a pig nearby to indicate the nature of the meat. Daubeny signified his pleasure at the gift, and after much smiling and hand-shaking on both sides, the men of Laripa withdrew, pleased that he was not offended, and doubled up with laughter at the trick they had played on him.

Daubeny and his companions roasted the meat on an im-promptu fire, ate it with some tinned asparagus, and spent a thor-oughly uncomfortable night, since they had virtuously come with-out carriers and only had one blanket apiece. The next day, Daubeny decided to return to Ungabunga. Though delighted by the kindness and hospitality of the Moroks, it was clear that, culturally, they re-sponded better to physical demonstration than to lectures. And al-though the prospect of repeating his dramatic gesture in every village of the Moroks was sufficiently disgusting to gratify even Daubeny's hunger for self-abasement, the response was likely to be emotional, and therefore unpredictable. Caution dictated that he should set up a model farm at Ungabunga, so that he could demonstrate his prin-ciples in a practical way. Dr. Prout wasn't going to like it, but he would understand, though Treadwell would certainly have it in for him. He cringed in anticipation of those contemptuous eyes in that great purple face, radiating the spiritual pride of a man who imagines himself to be a victim of society.

For several days after the departure of Daubeny and his companions, Garang went off to his rock overlooking the foaming waters of the Loma river with his favorite pig Naibiri. What was the Hidden Meaning of the Unmentionable Act? On the fourth day of his cogitations, when he thought the darkness of his mind would last for ever, he felt a tingling in his calves, his fingers twitched, his head reeled, and illumination burst upon him.

Of course! The secret of the red man's Unmentionable Act lay in the Houses of Filth that the men of Laripa had been commanded to build. The red men were no fools—they had power and wealth beyond the wildest dreams of his ancestors. So why should they store in their Houses of Filth what even fools could see was better thrown away? The young red man had given them the answer when he held up the filth in his own hands and told them it would turn into riches. If the True Men built these houses, as similar to those of the red men as possible, one day they would find, at the bottom of the holes, that their own filth had turned into riches: heaps and heaps of money, and jars of brilliantine, and lolly water, and sunglasses, and pressure lanterns, and radios, and motor-bikes!

From his crag, all his faculties exhausted, Garang surveyed his world with a new serenity. Archimedes in his bath, and Newton beneath the apple tree, had both felt that same exhilaration when they had pierced the veil of transitory things, and alone among men first saw reality for what it was. Like Garang, they had experienced the serenity of the true philosopher. Compared with this final revelation, his identification of Oelrichs as Oburabu, and his successful testing of the Father of Nyikang were minor theorems, mere lemmas.

Calling Naibiri to him, Garang made his way back to the village with the slow, deliberate steps of a prophet certain of his prophecy.

Some days later, the Mission staff at Ungabunga were startled by a deputation from Laripa, eagerly demanding to be instructed in latrine building. Daubeny was more than restored to favor with Prout by this turn of events, and even Treadwell grudgingly conceded that Daubeny might have the makings of a useful citizen. For three days the men of Laripa were diligently instructed in the finer points of privy building, and Daubeny, throwing caution aside, even showed them the advanced techniques of the four-holer, though Prout had to give him a little fatherly advice about not letting his pupils run before they could walk.

Just before they returned to Laripa, the men came to Daubeny and asked him when the filth would make riches for them. Taking the question to be a clumsy reference to the fertilising period of manure, he informed them that about eight months to a year would give excellent results. They seemed highly encouraged by this news and set off back to their village, laden with toilet rolls and lavatory chains to embellish their new Houses of Filth.

Within a few days, Houses of Filth began springing up like toadstools all over the mountains. Some were tall and spindly, raised on piles and very draughty; some were dark and cavernous sheds, whose sepulchral gloom was designed to spare the blushes of the users; some were plain and bleak, while others were richly ornamented and bedecked with lewd motifs. Most had pink-handled lavatory chains hanging outside, like inn-signs, and users wrapped toilet paper round their heads to signify that they had recently contributed to the common weal. For a person to defecate alone in the bush was now regarded as highly anti-social, selfishly depriving the community of who knew how many tins of talcum powder, or motor-bikes, or bottles of lolly-water.

Mothers brought their children to the nearest House of Filth at all hours of the day. Husbands now upbraided wives if they found them engaged in trivial household tasks. "Why are you not making riches for us in the House of Filth?" they shouted, hitting them with lumps of wood. The old men muttered cantankerously about the lack of public spirit nowadays among young people, who thought so little of their village that they could manage only one visit a day to the House of Filth. Tribal herbalists were pestered for simples to ease the bowels, and in one dreadful week, the villages of Mivana and Tolava were both blighted with constipation by the sorcerers of Niovoro, who were clearly intent on stealing the future wealth of their victims, since the Niovoro had been simultaneously blessed with dysentery. The great House of Filth at Niovoro was burnt to the ground as a reprisal, and a sorcerer lynched, and things gradually returned to normal.

The Lavalava, whom all the Moroks agreed were a bit odd, decided to dig the deepest hole of any village in the mountains at Abuk's instigation. For two months they toiled with buckets, picks, shovels, and crowbars supplied by the Mission. At the end of that time, they were down eighty feet, and without knowing it had built the mightiest throttling pit in the southern hemisphere. Its acoustic properties were remarkable, and even the tiniest child, held in its mother's hands, could wake strange echoes, while full-bellied males released eruptions and reverberations of volcanic thunder that stunned the waiting queue outside. This great pit was named "Voice of Oburabu," the great pig of Tikame, who, as well as being Mr. Oelrichs, was also believed to root and snort in the bowels of the earth. When Abuk felt irritable and out of sorts he would drive away the queue, and sit alone above the void, dreaming of grandeur.

Chapter X

AFTER CHRISTMAS the rain settled heavily over the island. Even down at Ungabunga they awoke at dawn every day to the sound of water dripping from the roofs and bushes, and found themselves blanketed in cold drizzling mist that restricted visibility to twenty yards. The paths were noisome and slippery underfoot, and the streams that fed the station roared day and night, swirling away down the drainage ditches beside the airstrip. Rainfall that season was the heaviest it had been for twenty years, and the sun showed itself only every week or so for a few hours, usually in the forenoon, before the clouds came down again.

In the high ranges behind the station, the rain was heavier, and the mists lay even thicker. The people were depressed, with many cases of flu and running noses, and as their spirits understandably drooped, they sought the release that tradition prescribed. A small party of warriors would slip away into the forest to seek a victim, perhaps wandering in search of a stray pig, and stalked him under the dripping trees until the moment came to loose their arrows and fall upon the outnumbered wretch. Seldom a week passed without an anguished scream of terror and agony suddenly breaking the silence of the valleys.

The rains caused numerous landslides on the track, making it impassable to horses and motorbikes. Even foot travellers, in moments of carelessness when picking their way over these obstacles, might set them sliding again, and be carried shrieking into the depths in a welter of rocks and mud and tree-roots. Nothing was ever found of such wayfarers except an occasional arm or other bloody fragments. Even Fletcher's patrols were reduced in the worst of the rainy season, unless there were specific reports of unusual mayhem, in which case he would dragoon the people and keep them busy clearing the slides. But this year he had every incentive to stay at home and allow the Moroks to do their worst.

What deterred Fletcher was insurmountable to the Mission, who hardly stirred from Ungabunga during the first three months of the new year, except for brief trips to the group of villages at Ramanu near the station. As they looked up into the mists, hardly daring to think of what the rumours hinted at, they were quietly relieved at having been overwhelmed by the problems of their own internal organization. Their children needed a school, and a paediatrician, since the clerks alone now numbered forty-seven, divided among nine departments, not to mention the extra personnel of the Library, the Gas Works, the Sex Education Clinic, the Printing Shop, and Telecommunications. The houses had begun developing the problems of houses everywhere—blocked waste-pipes, drawers that wouldn't shut, squeaking floorboards, and so on—and needed more and more attention.

The Printing Shop was worked to capacity, sixteen hours a day since, as Prout had explained, the onset of the big rains had given them all the opportunity to gather their strength for the great leap forward of the coming dry season. A torrent of official forms, questionnaires, departmental stationery, receipt books and registers streamed from the presses, and rapidly became the inflated currency of inter-departmental communication. By the beginning of March, the overworked clerks, many of whose wives acted as typists, were producing such a volume of correspondence, minutes, and memoranda that each department needed a full-time messenger to distribute the material to other departments, and by April, space had to be found in the largest store-shed for an archives section.

Treadwell rather welcomed the rains, since they helped him concentrate his energies on the instruction of his apprentices in the workshop. Under the gaslight, which evoked the atmosphere of heroic nineteenth-century proletarian struggle, he took his lads through pipefitting, welding, brazing, soldering, the use of testing apparatus, and the maintenance of standard appliances. But the daemonic ambience of the Moroks, which permeated Ungabunga, made it impossible to confine his thoughts and energies within the narrow syllabus of the City and Guilds Certificate for gas fitters. Fleeting visions of priapic lust would stay his hand as he was about to demonstrate the swaging of a joint, or the setting of the dies for tapping a thread, and he would throw down the tool of the moment and pace to and fro by the window, gazing out on the mountains and forests, only half aware of the noise of the torrents that roared ceaselessly around the Mission.

One evening, after demolishing half-a-dozen beers in morose isolation at the bar of the Cosmopolitan, he took his usual stroll through the mists which glowed at intervals from the new gaslights overhead, along the path that led him past the Puss-Puss shop, which Miss Gudrun Holmstrom had insisted be maintained as a therapeutic service for the Moroks. He was a familiar figure to the girls, who sensed the interest in his sly glances, and the tension that quivered in his squat body. Tonight the boss-girl, known to all the station as Tessie the Tub, had just stumped across the verandah to pitch the contents of a chamber-pot over the side. Something in the curve of her muscular forearm as she wielded the utensil fascinated Treadwell, and he turned with slow deliberation and made his way over to the steps.

Tessie's girls approached their job with the cheerful pragmatism of garage mechanics, and they were just about as handsome. The ponderous arrival of the distinguished white man consequently worked much the same transformation upon their demeanour as when the owner of a Rolls-Royce pulls into a rural gas station. Before Treadwell knew it, a dozen hands had smoothed his scanty hair, undone his tie and carefully folded it, and taken off his jacket. The proprietress of the service station herself led the guest to the only armchair, decorated with an ornamental rug thrown over the back and seat, and tossed some lumps of resinous gum onto the charcoal brazier in the centre of the room that sent up clouds of smoke, making Treadwell's eyes smart and begin to run. Taking a stubby of beer from a dirty enamel bowl full of water, she removed the cap with the end of a broken bayonet and handed it to him, after rubbing her hand round its mouth to clean it.

Now that he had broken the restraints of respectability, Treadwell felt rather at a loss and began swigging the sickly, tepid beer to hide his embarrassment.

"What girl you want fuck-fuck?" said Tessie, brightly—she prided herself on her English—and several girls sidled towards him out of the smoke, and began to unbutton their cotton gowns. Treadwell decided that the Morok smile was, if anything, even more unnerving than the Morok scowl. But the incense, the evening's liquor, and the carnal movements of the girls sufficiently inflamed his vital processes that he tore off his shirt and trousers, and finally attained his erotic goal, which was to grovel in his woollen underwear before the stalwart figure of Tessie the Tub.

The girls, dumbfounded by his posture and not grasping his Pidgin, began to clutch each other and giggle, but Tessie had seen service on more distant battlefronts, and silenced them by her demand for fifty dollars for the service.

On Treadwell's eager acquiescence, she tore the leg off a table and began to belabour him like an old carpet, abusing him hideously the while, a refinement of her trade she had picked up from one of her gentlemen in Nouméa, a crazed French lepidopterist. The girls skipped aside as the two went to it, Treadwell writhing in delicious submission under the blows, his shrieks of lust mingling with Tessie's oaths. The lovers' first encounter was finally ended when they collided with a wardrobe, one of whose legs was missing, which toppled on top of them. Treadwell was the first to disentangle himself from the wreckage, and found himself draped in one of Tessie's voluminous cotton print gowns. With porcine grunts he began pulling it over his head, groping with gnarled, spatulate fingers for the armholes.

Meanwhile, in the barracks, Trooper Gumbo had been promoted to corporal and accordingly, in the natural order of things, had spent the evening drinking himself into a fit with his mates. He had just gone outside for a hurl, and was wiping his chin afterwards, when the orgiastic noises from the Puss-Puss shop dawned upon his reeling brain. Thinking that a visit there would be a fitting conclusion to his revels, he moved unsteadily across the grass, and clambered up the steps just as Treadwell pulled the hem of his frock around his ankles and was looking coyly around him in anticipation of further delights.

Cpl Gumbo couldn't believe his luck. Through the smoke, dimly lit by the glow from the brazier, a vision of opulent female charms beckoned to him, which in reality was Treadwell in his baggy dress, teetering in a pair of Tessie's shoes, about to prostrate himself for the last time. The corporal, moustache bristling, in a few swift strides was at "her" side and, folding her in his arms had planted a lingering kiss on Treadwell's beer-stained and equally hairy mouth.

Astonished and horrified, the corporal flung Treadwell from him with a bellow of rage, while Treadwell kicked off his heels, gathered up his skirts, and made for the door. Cpl Gumbo was not far behind, determined to obliterate the monstrosity that had just shaken his simple world to its foundations, but Treadwell had a few seconds' start, and, less drunk than Gumbo, legged it in fine style towards the Mission with the corporal lurching and braying for vengeance through the mists. By a process of blundering miscalculation Treadwell suddenly found himself outside the Prouts' door, which he recognized by some dying hollyhocks that Phyllis had tried to grow. Battering on the door, he called for aid, and Prout let him in a few seconds before the arrival of the corporal, who promptly began kicking at the panels.

The thunderous row attracted the notice of Fletcher, Oelrichs and Moncreif, who were strolling back from the Cosmopolitan, and out of curiosity rather than from any desire to be helpful, they wandered over to enjoy what looked to be a promising piece of entertainment.

It took a swinging cuff to the head before Gumbo finally half-came to his senses and told Fletcher of the monstrous apparition that had attacked him in the Puss-Puss shop. Fletcher was about to put the drunken oaf on a charge for lying to a superior officer when Prout, hearing Fletcher's voice, opened the door and querulously asked him to have the goodness to maintain better discipline among his men. Discomfited, Fletcher began hauling Gumbo away when Moncreif, who was standing at an angle so that he could see into the hall behind Prout, noticed a wisp of female garment protruding from a closet door.

"Well Roger, whatever kind of Amazon it was that frightened the shit out of Gumbo, she's in there all right—look at that!"

"Strewth, yer right. Just what the hell *have* you got in there, Prout?" Rudely pushing past him, they entered the hall and wrenched open the closet door, to reveal Treadwell struggling to remove a suspender belt entangled round his knees.

It was some time before the plane could get in, but on Friday morning the pilot said he'd give it a go. Treadwell, together with the loyal members of the Mission, including the Prouts, was sitting by the edge of the strip with his gear in readiness for the plane, when Fletcher and the sergeant-major walked by.

"Cheer up, Obadiah," said Fletcher. "When yer get 'ome the Poms'll make yer a Sir—it's all the rage over there."

Chapter XI

ARLY IN APRIL Prout called his staff together to explain the campaign of liberation that was to begin as soon as the roads were passable.

"We've all been feeling the strain during the past few months, so this is a good opportunity to reassure you that after all the solid teamwork we've put into this job, we are about to reap the reward of our labours. The backbone of our programme is the new constitution, which will be ratified on Independence Day. I'll ask Mr Moncreif to give us an outline of the constitution that he and I have drawn up, beginning with the Bill of Rights."

Moncreif tilted back his chair, and expatiated.

"I'm sure we all want to give these admirable people their rightful deserts, so I can assure you that we have ransacked the world's treasuries of political wisdom on their behalf. To begin with, let us consider the Bill of Rights. The Elephant Island Constitution is based on the self-evident principles that the inhabitants of have an inalienable right to aid from the over-privileged nations; to immunity from the provisions of international law, which has been developed by and for the benefit of those over-privileged nations; and to immunity from all insensitive and hostile criticisms of their internal affairs by those nations. I'm sure you will all agree that this is an essential foundation for the dignity and self-respect of the indigenes."

He paused, and sensed Prout's suspicion, as well as the air of hostile uneasiness which pervaded the meeting. He pressed on, enjoying every minute of it.

"The Bill of Rights itself assumes, of course, that the natural aims of all human life are the joys of creative endeavour, brotherly love, and self-sacrifice, and that all distinctions of race, tribe, sex, age, height, strength, and intelligence are the reactionary fantasies of an oppressive ideology, lacking any foundation in scientific fact. All laws violating these truths will naturally be unconstitutional and void. On this foundation we have erected the following institutional structure. There will be two Co-Presidents, without powers of veto, to hold office for a year, and to be elected at half-yearly intervals, so that each Co-President will only hold office for six months with any other. There will be elected assemblies for the village, the catchment area, and the Island, with a two-chamber legislature at the apex of the hierarchy, comprising a House of Deputies and a Senate, each of which will be able to veto the legislation of the other. The constituency of the House of Deputies will be the catchment area, which will also be the constituency of the Senate, but in the case of the Senate voters will cast their ballots for a single national slate. All voting will naturally be by proportional representation. There will be no qualifications of any kind for voters or the members of any elected body, since that would create invidious and unconstitutional distinctions. Elephant Island will thus be in advance of every other democracy in the world, since an infant's drool on the ballot paper will be, in every respect, the equal of an adult's dirty thumbprint. Thus age discrimination and the historical oppression of babies is ended at a stroke."

The silence was frigid, and he went on, unperturbed.

"Judges will also be elected to the local courts, the Court of Appeal, and the Supreme Court, but here again any provision for special qualifications would be invidious and divisive, and violate the Bill of Rights. No elitist notions of literacy here, you will be pleased to observe. Oh yes, I forgot to say that all voting will take place once a year. How does that strike you?"

"You will, of course," said Prout, acidly, "disregard the frivolous and mischievous manner in which Moncreif has seen fit to present the Constitution, and which we might have expected of him. In fact, the Bill of Rights will simply be the United Nations Declaration of Human Rights, of which we have been given a most malicious parody. But the basic information he has presented on the institutional framework of the Constitution is correct. What do you all feel about the political structures of the Constitution?"

"Well," said Daubeny, "It all seems rather authoritarian to me. The people are really being forced and regimented into a most rigid form of system."

"That's right, man," said Richie Kleist, the Cultural Development Officer, from Ottawa. He was an obese young man, with rimless glasses, thick lips, and a goatee, with spindly legs that flew in all directions as he walked, as though collapsing under his weight. His favorite topic of conversation was his exertions on behalf of pimps and drug pushers in the slums of Toronto. "These guys have been pushed around too goddamn much. They need air to breathe, to swing their balls around, after twenty thousand years of shit an' oppression."

"If I may say so," Prout broke in, "I think you are all mistaking the real aim of this Constitution. It has been designed precisely to allow the maximum possible opportunities for self-expression by the people, hence the elaborate apparatus of checks and balances. What we have provided is simply the canvas and the frame within which the people may draw their own vision of their future, the basic tool kit with which they can express their aspirations for that new way of life which they so much desire."

This high-minded defense did much to quell suspicion of the constitution, which, sprang less from its contents than from the fact that Moncreif had had a major hand in it. But Prout's testimony showed it to be the liberal-minded conception that it truly was.

After some technical arguments about its production and dissemination, Prout declared, "The people can ratify their new Constitution on Independence Day, which in my view should be July 14th. This is Bastille Day, of course, which I think very appropriate for a people who have been deprived of their rights for so long."

The assembled company all nodded vigorously, as if to indicate they not only knew what Bastille Day was, but had been about to suggest it themselves.

"It will take about three months for us to get everything organized, and that date will also fall in the middle of the dry season. I have also heard from the Chairman of the Committee on Decolonisation, Lord Southall, that he'll be able to visit us in July, so the 14th will be ideal in every way. As you probably all know, Lord Southall is not only an economist but also one of the world's foremost champions of human rights, and only last year persuaded the Catatonian Government to abolish prisons, for which he has just been awarded the Jenkins Prize for Social Compassion." Prout did not add that the miserable republic of Catatonia had since been almost dismembered by blood feuds, private armies, and trade-union intimidation.

Lord Southall, although only a Life Peer, came from a family with distinguished, not to say aristocratic, Liberal antecedents; starting life as an economist, he had gone to the United Nations as an adviser on development programmes and never looked back. His intellectual convictions, born of years of study, and his deep awareness of suffering humanity, gave him a moral force that none could resist as he charted his course of rescue among the developing nations of the world with absolute assurance. But by some strange process that defied analysis, his touch upon the nations he came to save reliably sent them into a rapid social decline: ancient African kingdoms were dismembered by civil war; robust republics of Amerindian peasants were reduced to beggary overnight; Muslim emirates were plunged into anarchy and despair. His genial self-confidence, and his reputation, grew with every disaster, as the expiring victims of his benevolence strewed his career like water-logged hulks in the wake of some pocket-battleship.

"Of course," Prout was saying, "his advice on such an occasion will be invaluable, and I've no doubt we shall all learn a great deal. It's also a way of reassuring those of us who are feeling a little remote from the centre of things that those who matter are thinking about us. So, let's put our backs into it over the next three months to show them their trust in us has not been misplaced. Now, Tristram, what was it you wanted to raise?"

"Well, Dr. Prout, I think we've all heard these horrible rumours about killings up in the mountains, and even cannibalism. They seem such kind people that I can't believe they're true, but oughtn't we to investigate, in case something's gone wrong somehow?"

"I quite agree, and as soon as we can persuade the people to open the roads we'll send up a welfare team. But we must be prepared for a temporary increase in violence at this stage of the process which we are inducing. We are passing through a phase of transitional disequilibrium, in which a centrifugal shift of the locus of interaction is producing a redeployment of social forces."

His audience looked a little blank. He tried again.

"Inevitably, when one releases pressure built up under a colonial regime, and transfers power back to the local communities, the old equilibrium will take time to re-establish itself. As you know, before the white man disturbed the social system, there would have been relatively little fighting, but the suppression of the traditional mechanisms which maintained social solidarity built up tensions which must now dissipate, and that is what is happening at the moment. But as soon as they ratify the Constitution and realise that they are their own masters, and that they are free to compose their differences peacefully again, we can expect to see a marked decrease in violence. You see, it was precisely *because* the old regime prevented the people settling their disputes themselves, and forced them to go to the government, that violence was produced, in fact encouraged! The old regime systematically ordered the people to fight one another, as you know—indeed, the first thing I saw when I arrived was a battle on the airstrip—and then went so far as to claim that it was maintaining law and order! At the same time, it destroyed the people's self-respect by brutal oppression that reduced them to the status of a degraded proletariat. The twin forces of the loss of self-respect and government intervention in their disputes has naturally led to a temporary disposition towards greater violence."

Everyone looked immensely relieved by this cogent analysis of indigenous violence, except Moncreif, who acidly commented, "I wasn't aware that the *ancien régime* had instructed the people in cannibalism." Prout turned on him with waspish impatience:

"If anyone had ever instructed *you* in the rudiments of anthropology, Moncreif, you would know that ninety-nine percent of the stories of cannibalism are based on the racial prejudices of missionaries and traders, as a justification of their barbarous treatment of indigenous peoples, and they have absolutely no foundation in fact. The remaining one percent can be accounted for as the ritual sharing of small pieces of their loved ones. Perfectly natural. I don't find that any more disgusting than a Catholic who believes he is eating the body of Christ. You've been carried away by those imperialist fantasies of your friend Fletcher, I'm afraid. There's simply no evidence that these people are cannibals."

"Yes, you should try and get out among the real people a bit more, Moncreif," said Daubeny. "I did, and found that I much profited by the experience."

"Quite," said Prout. "Now, we have a few other items before lunch."

That night, as Phyllis poured the Nescafé after supper, there was a tapping on the fly-screen door. Sydney went to investigate—they kept no servants, of course—and found Snail Slime lurking outside, looking even more furtive and venomous than usual. Prout, however, saw him as a humble but sincere campaigner for social justice for his people, and the victim of Fletcher's unspeakable brutality on his first patrol. He welcomed him inside and introduced him to Phyllis, who already knew of his sufferings on that infamous patrol, and sat him down and brought him cakes and coffee. Snail Slime tucked his feet under his chair, curling his toes, demolished the cakes with both hands, took one mouthful of the coffee and spat it back in the cup, and said he wanted to tell big fellow master about how liklik fellow master had "cook him house belong all fellow kanaka."

Prout beamed upon him, like Diogenes on the point of discovering a just man, and fetched some beer from the kitchen. At first Snail Slime was cautious, testing the extent of Prout's knowledge, and only suggested that liklik fellow master had "cook him house, bugger up him garden, kill him pig belong all fellow kanaka." But as he discovered that Prout could hear nothing bad enough about Fletcher, his desire to please a superior, his feculent imagination, and his thirst for vengeance against Fletcher for that knuckle sandwich ten months prior loosened all restraints, and he embarked on a saga of lust and cruelty that would have made Caligula weep.

By the end of five stubbies, Snail Slime had transformed the syl-
van glens of Elephant Island into a reeking shambles in which the
burning alive of piccaninnies in houses, the bayoneting of pregnant
women, and the ravishing of old people were the commonplaces
of everyday life at the hands of Fletcher and the fiends under his
command. For three hours, Snail Slime basked in the horrified fas-
cination of Sydney and Phyllis, and at the end of his story he asked
them, gleefully:

"You kill him liklik master die finish?"

Prout laboriously explained that first there must be big talk-
talk along court house, and then the white men over the sea would
put him in the calaboose, cut him grass till him die finish. Snail
Slime was crestfallen to discover that no bloodier end was in store
for Fletcher, but realised that the red men could not be expected to
kill one of their own kind for the benefit of the True Men. He became openly alarmed, however, when he learned that he would be
expected to appear in court personally, to provide names and dates
and, preferably, witnesses to substantiate his lies. Phyllis went out to
the kitchen to make some more coffee, while Snail Slime sat looking
at the floor, twisting his legs still further under the chair.

"Why does he look so frightened, dear?" she asked, as she returned with the tray. "Could he be afraid that Fletcher will try to
murder him?"

Prout reassured him that he would be absolutely safe under the
protection of the Mission, and that this applied to his witnesses as
well. At length he seemed to recover his confidence, and promised
to return in a few days with some witnesses to substantiate his story.

After he had slipped out into the darkness, Sydney and Phyllis
sat together before the gas-fire, for the cloudless night was unusually
chilly, and held one another's hands in silence. A tear ran slowly
down her cheek, and Prout leaned over and kissed her tenderly. She

fell into his arms, clutching him desperately as a shield against the horrors of this world and sobbing bitterly as he caressed her golden hair. She ran her fingers up and down his bony vertebrae and he put his hand under her chin, tilting back her head so that her plump lips were upturned to meet his, and she overbalanced, pulling him on top of her.

He began fumbling at her blouse...

Chapter XII

ABUK WAS DISENCHANTED. It was all very well digging riches from the Houses of Filth, but Laripa and that twisted little monster Garang would get all the credit. In fact, they had got it already. The men of Laripa had put on a definite swagger since the Great Revelation swept the mountains, and were not only claiming the right to instruct everyone else in the building of Houses of Filth, but also a share in the proceeds. Things had gone far enough; Lavalava needed a Counter-Revelation to give one in the eye to Laripa and even the score. Tired of brooding on ways his people had been wronged, Abuk had come down to Ungabunga with his wives to sell vegetables and some meat, and buy a few odds and ends in Erny's store. This had greatly expanded since the arrival of the Mission, keeping Erny so busy that now he was only drunk by the late afternoon.

There had been a tremendous rush for brilliantine, chewing gum, perfume, baby powder to make their skins shine, lipstick, sunglasses, synthetic gold-lamé shawls, and cow-boy boots, and after a visit to the store the dreaded warriors who had stalked into Ungabunga naked and predatory would totter back into the mountains on their high heels, reeking of jasmine, veiled and peering bashfully at a rose-tinted world like a bevy of Levantine harlots.

Abuk was astounded by the changes at Ungabunga since his last visit the year before, when he had led Lavalava against Niovoro on the day of Prout's arrival. Where the old fort once dominated the station now stood the great orange cylinders of the Gas Works, and the cluster of store-sheds. The residences of Fletcher and Oelrichs were untouched on the hillside above the Gas Works, but below it the older buildings had been submerged in a flood of asbestos-walled prefabricated mediocrity. Only the Cosmopolitan Hotel breasted the tide, looming like a Mississippi stern-wheeler over a flock of cabin cruisers. On the airstrip and the rough ground outside the store fretful, anaemic, red-eyed European children, with pasty skin inflamed by sun and fungal infections, snivelled and wrangled like village dogs over the possession of scooters, pedal-cars, and dolly-prams.

Abuk sent his wives to the scale to sell their vegetables, and walked over to the store. He beamed at two blue-eyed urchins who stood outside the door, for like all the Moroks he loved children. It was strange to him that the red men's children should be so discontented and unhappy, when they had so much, but then, who could understand anything about the red men? The Morok children were cheerful, yet more mature even as toddlers; while the Morok boys dashed off into the forest to hunt small game with bows and arrows, their serious-faced sisters followed their mothers to work dutifully in the gardens with miniature string bags.

As he stepped through the new glass doors, into the gas-lit interior, with its vinyl-tiled floor, formica-topped counters, glass and chrome display cases that had replaced the rough old boards and fly-blown shelves of last year, his jaw dropped.

"Ekeh! Ekeh! Ekeh!" he intoned in wonder, and for the next half-hour he wandered round the displays of merchandise with the innocent curiosity of a child. Erny had been trying out some new lines of goods, including toys for the European children, and found that model cars, lorries, bulldozers and other vehicles sold very well.

Eventually Abuk came around to these and paused, attracted by their bright colors but without the slightest conception of their use. It was early in the afternoon, business was slack, and Erny was sober, bored, and looking for some diversion. Noting Abuk's interest, he spent the next twenty minutes showing him how the cars would run by themselves after they had been wound up or their wheels were rotated by friction. Abuk was entranced and soon had every vehicle out on the counter, running them in all directions. He suggested that they were the red men's versions of baby pigs, and Erny, who was just starting on his second bottle, and in an increasingly loquacious mood, explained that in his country these things were so big that real people could sit inside them and be carried about. Abuk was almost as astonished by this information as he had been to see the toys move by themselves, and when his women finally came in to join him, he purchased a Lincoln Continental and went out clutching it.

Over the next few days he played with his new car for hours every day, even neglecting his visits to the House of Filth, and was always surrounded by a fascinated audience. One night, he dreamed that his old father, long dead, was still alive, and that he contemptuously flung the car away into a nearby garden. After a time, a strange disturbance was seen beneath the soil, and suddenly with a roar a vast shiny metal object heaved itself out of the ground, shaking off the dirt in showers. It was a real Lincoln Continental, the size of a house, and stood there making a loud whizzing noise. He and his father got in, and were both carried to Laripa where they drove through the stockade with a crash of splintering timber and roared up and down the dance-yard, scattering the inhabitants like chickens. As they were about to ram the great men's house he woke up. It was still dark outside. As he lay there and recalled the details of the dream, he realised that it was the Sign for which he had been waiting, the much-needed Counter-Revelation.

Erny was astonished when a couple of days later a body of Abuk's kinsmen descended on his store and bought every toy vehicle he possessed. So clamorous were they that he dug out some of his old stock of simple models that had no means of propulsion, but these were indignantly flung down when the Moroks discovered this deficiency, flashing dark, suspicious glances from under their heavy brows at the unfortunate Erny, who promised to radio for a larger stock as soon as possible. Phyllis Prout, and Cyril's wife, Noreen Hiscock, were in the store while the savage Moroks clamoured for toys, a scene to melt the heart of any woman.

"Would you believe it?" said Noreen, "Aren't they sweet?"

"Yes, when you hear all that's said about them, and you see something like this, it's just wonderful, and heartwarming!"

"I remember last Christmas in Sydney, before we came here, Cyril and I went down to David Jones, to buy some prezzies for our two youngest, it was *just* the same, *just* the same."

The two women beamed at the Morok men as they trailed out of the store with their boxes of toys. Erny came over to serve them, mopping his brow.

"Strewth, I dunno what's got into 'em, Phyllis. Cleaned me flamin' stock right out! Never thought I'd be cablin' for a ton o' clockwork toys. Still, it's good for business. Now, what can I get yer?"

Prout was equally delighted by the news.

"What's so remarkable is that the conception of toys for children is a very sophisticated idea. Of course, children everywhere make playthings of natural materials, but in this case their parents are actually spending hard-earned money in buying these toys. That's what is so encouraging. It shows that even our most advanced ideas can be communicated across the barriers of culture and education. Did you know that a number of villages have actually *asked* Schultz to build them village halls?"

"That's just wonderful, dear. But Erny's having trouble getting all the toys they need. It seems a shame that we can't help airlift toys and sweeties to the kiddies."

Prout put his mind to work on this, and it was arranged that the Mission would give Erny a guaranteed price for his entire stock of toys, and would undertake distribution themselves. And it was fortunate that such arrangements were being made, since up in the mountains, events were moving rapidly. At Lavalava several yielding gardens were uprooted, and the men planted their first crop of bakers' vans, steam-rollers, double-decker buses, fire-engines, petrol-tankers, Mercedes, and Lincoln Continentals. Around the men's house, Abuk had planted a private herbaceous border of fork-lift trucks and bulldozers. It was held that only men could plant the new crop, which counted as yams in their cosmology, and were therefore taboo to women.

The news of Lavalava's discovery spread rapidly in the mountains. Their neighbours, who shared their resentment of the overweening claims of Laripa, were delighted that men of the Tolava valley should have evened the score with the inflated pigs' bladders inhabiting the Loma valley, and it was seriously debated if the Houses of Filth might not be a completely bogus revelation. After all, could something that violated every canon of decency truly be a means of insight? The practical replied that these philosophical quibbles were all very well, but since Lavalava had what was indisputably the finest House of Filth in the land of the Moroks, it would be absurd not to continue using it. Moreover, since the red men obviously had many means of obtaining their wealth, both Revelations might be true.

Garang and the men of Laripa treated the Revelation of the

Lavalava with the contempt of a Cathedral Dean and Chapter for the home-made prophecies of a Welsh tabernacle. But while most of the villages in the Laripa area publicly shared this contempt, numerous men planted secret plots of toys in the forest, tying them in yam vines, and muttering their private spells upon them.

The huge consignment of toys chartered by Erny also proved fortunate for the Mission, since toys and tobacco were the only currency that the Moroks would accept now for clearing the landslides. Fletcher would have refused to let his police enforce road clearing even if he had been asked, and in the absence of any other means of coercion, bribery, of oriental proportions, the terms of which increased daily, was the only course open to the Mission.

The end of the rains produced a fine crop of respiratory diseases, and Smith was anxious to take a medical patrol on the newly-opened roads. Prout gave permission for the natives to be allowed to carry as volunteers, since this was a medical patrol. Smith persuaded a few surly men from Ramanu to carry the boxes of penicillin, distilled water vials, and syringes and other equipment in exchange for a pound of tobacco a day. When Prout heard of this, he indignantly insisted that they be given free blankets, hurricane lamps, shirts and trousers, as well as chits for a case of bully-beef, redeemable at the store, and told Smith that even a medical patrol must be careful not to take the indigenes' help for granted.

On the patrol, the carriers flung many of the cartons over the side of the track before the eyes of Smith, but presented themselves empty-handed at the end of the day to demand their tobacco, with expressions of insufferable insolence. The slightest delay in meeting their rancorous demands for payment was received with abuse and threatening gestures. The chiefs of every village through which the patrol passed demanded further payments of tobacco for the privilege of using the road, and their men pillaged many of the remaining cartons to extract aluminum foil, which they rolled up and stuck through their noses, and tubes of ointment, which they used for greasing their skins.

In spite of this harassment, the patrol treated several hundred people, and Smith returned after three weeks with a sense of considerable achievement. He then discovered that the station had been besieged by angry Moroks demanding compensation for their injuries at the hands of the doctor, when he stuck the needle into them, and the Mission had been obliged to make a distribution of cooking pots to send them away peacefully. When Smith protested that the people were not only conspicuously ungrateful for having their sickness cured, but had done their best to make the patrol downright impossible, Prout replied, with a smile.

"Why *should* they be grateful? They have a *right* to free medical attention. Gratitude belongs to the era of exploitation when they grovelled to their white masters for every scrap they condescended to toss them. It's clear from what you say that they're only showing a healthy spirit of self-assertion."

"But to pay them, to give them cooking pots for being injected, for having their lives saved? It's madness, madness!"

"Not madness, Dr. Smith, but the utilization of a slight misunderstanding, a mistranslation of categories between two cultures, to spread the use of modern kitchen equipment among the people."

Smith showed a healthy spirit of self-assertion by losing his temper for the first time since coming to Elephant Island and resigning on the spot. The Moroks had, by now, all caught the scent of fear and weakness that exuded from the Mission, and it became great sport for each village to send down a party of extortioners to Ungabunga to cajole or intimidate the red men there into disgorging more of their wealth.

Delighted by their tactics in getting compensation for their injections, and finding that every ailment was treated with injections by the incompetent native orderlies flown in at short notice from other parts of the Pacific to take Smith's place, the Moroks poured in to the clinic groaning, rolling their eyes, hopping, staggering, and clutching various parts of their anatomy, all demanding succour. Some, more histrionically gifted than their fellows, caused themselves to be plastered with leaves and mud, and carried the last mile slung under poles, to be deposited outside the clinic, groaning and comatose. This always caused a rush of Mission wives, helping in the clinic, to ease their sufferings, and the sight of the red women gathered in pathetic distress around their patients was the source of endless hilarity back in the mountains, as they mimicked their fluttering concern.

Other natives favored a more direct approach, stalking grim-faced into the clinic and pointing to where they wished for the injection, menacing the orderlies horridly with their glittering axes.

From the clinic the Moroks streamed over to the warehouses to demand compensation for the pain of the injections, and for the injury to their dignity sustained thereby. The supply of cooking pots ran out after a fortnight, and the harassed clerks were driven to opening the first crates that came to hand, barely able to drag them out and get the lids off before the shouts and screams became deafening, and the Moroks flooded over the counter, to haul out the contents and spread them all over the floor in a debris of wood-shavings and shredded paper. Those who had had injections demanded twice as much as those who had simply come for what they could pick up, and some furious fights developed between the clinic patients and the casual scroungers.

One morning, shortly after the last of the book-binding kits had been given away, the duty clerk, one Terry Woodford, opened a crate of Japanese plastic clarinets, and was so incautious as to fit a reed to one and blow a few notes upon it. The Moroks, who had always made bamboo flutes, were astounded by these sweet notes, which, far from soothing their savage breasts, awoke in them a frenzy of avarice. Vaulting the counter, they fell upon the crate, whereupon Terry, a young lad who only wanted to oblige, opened two more. Some Scroungers, who had been first in the queue, tried to slip out with an armful of clarinets each, but were quickly spotted by the Patients, who pursued them across the station.

Fletcher was taking morning parade as usual, and had just completed his inspection when the mob burst onto the airstrip, where the Scroungers were finally outrun by the Patients and brought to bay. Surrounded, the Scroungers flung down their surplus instruments, and, swinging the remainder over their heads, tried to batter their way out of the encircling ring. The yells and thuds of battle grew louder as the laggards of both factions caught up, and soon the airstrip was filled with furiously angry little men thrashing one another with their new clarinets. The metal furniture proved an admirable reinforcement to the tough plastic, and capable of inflicting some gory wounds, though the instruments had the disconcerting habit of flying apart at the joints before the quietus could be given. Fletcher and his men sat on their horses, helpless with laughter, until Prout arrived in great agitation, hurrying down from a conference on the demographic characteristics of the Elephant Island population. He stared at the scene in uncomprehending dismay.

At this point the warriors were joined by reinforcements with flutes and cor anglais on the flanks, preceded by a heavy brigade in the van equipped with bassoons. One humourist had found some cymbals, and was prancing up and down the side of the strip with elephantine gaiety, clashing them furiously, and every now and then catching a straggler a dreadful slashing blow with an edge.

Fletcher rode over to Prout.

"What's this, then? The Ungabunga Philharmonic 'aving their first rehearsal?"

"Good God, Fletcher, it's appalling! I've never seen anything like it."

"What about the day yer first came here, then?"

"That was different. You'd encouraged them, given them weapons of war, but we're their *friends*, we've given them these beautiful instruments. They have some musical tradition, so how can they behave like this?"

"Don't ask me, mate. I'm just a kiap. Ye're the expert."

"You'll have to take your men down and make them see reason," said Prout, who realised that this was beyond even his powers of conciliation.

"I will, will I? Get stuffed!"

"Surely you will agree, Fletcher, that it's in everybody's interests to stop this! I can't order you to do so–"

Five frenzied Moroks, trundling a harp, now made their appearance. As the great instrument on its trolley gathered speed down the strip, which was hard and dry after several weeks of sun, it took on a momentum of its own, and leaving its keepers floundering in the rear it cut a swathe through the heaving mob, thrumming and jangling. The plangent chords blended harmoniously with the startled cries of pain, and several Moroks looked up vacantly, as though summoned by angels, in which rapturous posture they were felled by the bassoons of the heavy brigade.

Prout was wringing his hands like a pair of wet socks.

"Do something, Fletcher, do something, for Heaven's sake," he cried, distracted with grief and mortification. "You can't just stand by and watch these people kill each other."

"Can't I? Anyway, the killing hasn't started yet. They'll wear 'emselves out first. They usually do."

"You must be mad, Fletcher. You must stop them, by force, if necessary!"

"Ye're not tellin' me to bash yer brown brothers, are yer?"

"For Heaven's sake, don't sit there tormenting me, get on with it!" shrieked Prout.

Without more ado Fletcher formed up his men for a charge, and they fell on the combatants, firing over their heads with shotguns and laying about them with batons, and dispersed the mob in a few minutes with minor casualties. The Moroks were so exhausted that the sudden shock of the charge totally demoralised them, and they could offer little resistance. Fletcher dismissed his men, and rode back to where Prout was standing.

"Reckon yer learnin'! I told yer bayonets and a belt round the ear was what they understood."

Prout glared at him and walked off without saying another word.

Chapter XIII

C HIEF JUSTICE ROBINSON leaned forward across the mahogany desk and cupped his ear towards the witness in the box. He was a deliberately Dickensian figure, all whiskers, gold chains and seals, macassar oil, flashes of silk kerchief, and *pincenez*, with a large hooked nose and heavy rumpled jowls, ruminating suspiciously on every proposition advanced by witness or by counsel as though tasting it for some hidden poison.

His legal abilities were mediocre, and until only a month before he had been an aging barrister in Australia, something of a joke to his colleagues, and with no hope of ever becoming a judge. Perhaps his flamboyant dress and affectations were gestures of defiance to hide his professional disappointment; they certainly attracted the attention of those who were trying to find a temporary Chief Justice for Elephant Island. When they also heard of his moral fervour for black men they decided he was the obvious man for the job.

Being entirely humourless, he naturally assumed that his powers of mind and heart had finally been recognised, and until an indigene could be found to take his place, was determined to use his new position "to stamp out colonialism with a firm hand," as he put it. So it was much to his distress that the first case to come up before him, under the old Criminal Code of Elephant Island, which remained in force until the new constitution was ratified on Independence Day, was that of Ajang of Niovoro.

He was charged with the murder of three young girls in a hut behind the Cosmopolitan Hotel. They worked for Madame Negretti, and one Saturday afternoon while they were dozing in their little hut, Ajang surprised them and subdued them into silent, shrinking terror with his axe, raped them, hacked them to death, and then set fire to the hut, where their charred bodies were discovered after the blaze had been extinguished.

Running from the flames with his blood-stained axe, he had been intercepted by some of Fletcher's police who had engaged him in conversation about his recent relationship with the three girls, and the possibly psychological motivations of his pyromania, though naturally their language was not quite as sophisticated as this. At the end of their conversation they had taken him, unharmed, to Prout's residence and handed him over to the Commissioner and his wife. Sydney and Phyllis were consternated by the fellow's open admission of his guilt, since he had insisted on giving them a detailed description of how he had spent the gory afternoon.

Prout had put him on his honour to remain on the station until the Chief Justice's arrival, and Ajang promised faithfully that he would be as Father of Nyikang's little dog, following him everywhere. On the following afternoon, as he made his escape up the track from the station to go home to Niovoro, he had been ambushed by men from the girls' village and fled for his life, pelting back to the station with the avengers at his heels and only eluding them by suddenly veering off the track and bounding down a precipitous short cut of bare clay and slippery short grass that ended at the station.

And now, in the fine new Palace of Justice, he was to answer for his atrocious crimes. He had, with the rest of the Moroks, watched its recent completion, with its pentagonal glass tower that rose nearly as high as the Gas Works, and naturally believed it was the new and grander calaboose to replace the one destroyed on Prout's orders. If the red men were so anxious to build this great calaboose, what would they do to those they put inside it? The Moroks who saw it shrank inwardly with the fear of nameless imaginings.

The slate tablet above the tall bronze doors was intended to depict one of the major themes of modern justice. According to the UNESCO brochure, it depicted Justice redistributing wealth according to the Principle of Affirmative Action; unfortunately, to the artistically uninstructed, it appeared that a female with all the angular charm of a praying mantis had just snatched a cluster of *objets d'art* from a whimpering aesthete, and was about to bestow them on a clamorous horde of retarded delinquents.

The whole of the Mission's personnel, except a few mothers and children, had assembled in the main courtroom and were seated on the padded red cushions along the benches of fumed oak. Although they had been joined by a number of Moroks, anxious to see what peculiar torments the building was intended to provide, the court was still only three-quarters full.

The great room was acoustically perfect, sound-proof and double-glazed, with a ceiling lined with sound-absorbent tiles, and the dimensions computer-calculated to allow the mumblings of the most repressed or cleft-palated witness to reach the Judge's desk, which was raised above the floor by several steps. Naturally, the court was fully air-conditioned, and equipped with the latest sound-recording devices, with microphones at every strategic point. Connected by sound-proof doors was the Law Library, with a compendious selection of legal authorities from the English-speaking world, and especially strong in Admiralty and commercial law.

Sgt Oala was in the witness box, concluding his evidence on the flight of Ajang from the burning hut, and his subsequent confession to the police. Since the Chief Justice did not understand Pidgin, an interpreter from the Mission was necessary.

"Now," said the Judge, looking fiercely at the sergeant, "let us get to the bottom of this disgraceful affair. Do I understand that you not only apprehended the prisoner, but that you actually questioned him without advising him of his rights?"

"What rights?"

The Judge's *pince-nez* fell off with a plop on to the note-pad, and he blew his nose like a Pharaoh's trumpet.

"You prevaricate, Sergeant. I refer to his rights to be informed that he was not obliged to answer any questions you put to him, of course, and to have a solicitor present."

The sergeant looked puzzled, as well he might, for in the Statutes of Elephant Island there was no place for lawyers to help defendants dodge the sword of justice. This was because the Moroks regarded rape, arson, pillaging, malicious wounding, and homicide, not as crimes to be denied, or even to be excused as regrettable personal lapses, but as achievements to be celebrated and which brought renown to their families and villages. In the days before Fletcher, they received only modest terms of imprisonment even for murder, and the local jail had become a sort of club for exiled notables. So they liked nothing better than a court hearing where they could make speeches for hours about their heroic deeds, in endless and repulsive detail, to an audience of discerning red men. Suggestions by the Resident Magistrate that a particularly unpleasant atrocity might have been an accident, or possibly performed in self-defence, would be indignantly rejected as slurs on the manhood of the accused. These finer points of Morok jurisprudence were lost on the Chief Justice, however, who had comprehensively misunderstood the Statutes.

"But why is it good to tell a man he may keep silent, Sir, when you think he has done wrong?"

"Because it is not for ignorant men like you to say if a man has done wrong. That is for courts of law, for psychiatrists, for experts to decide. Leave the box! The evidence which you have given is worthless, and shall be disregarded." His outburst produced a paroxysm of coughing, and it was some time before he could continue.

"Dr. Prout," he wheezed at last, "will you kindly favor us with your evidence on this case?" Prout entered the witness box, and was sworn. "Now, please tell us all you know."

"Well, your Honour, I'm afraid that, while the sergeant's methods of extracting evidence were of course quite deplorable and inadmissible, the accused did give my wife and me a most minute and detailed description of the rape and murder of these young girls, and of how he used a drum of kerosene to burn the house."

"No doubt he did, no doubt he did," said the Judge, testily. "But have you reflected, Dr. Prout, that he was probably telling you all this while still in fear of his person after the interrogation he had just undergone? Had you considered that point, Dr Prout?"

"I must admit, that since he seemed quite composed, and in fact, almost eager to tell me the story, I thought he was speaking the truth, without compulsion."

"Compulsion, Dr. Prout?" He looked very hard at the Commissioner over his pince-nez. "If only you had had my years of experience in the courts, and in the intimidation of witnesses by the police, you would not use that word so lightly. It would amaze the layman to be told that compulsion may be exerted not only by the fist and the boot, but in the most insidious ways. Are you aware, Dr. Prout, that even a policeman drumming his fingers on a table for ten minutes can induce such a state of hypnotic terror in a suspect that he may confess to anything?"

"Bullshit!" roared Fletcher. "If he'd drummed on the bastard's head with a mallet for ten minutes he might 'a got somewhere."

"Silence! Silence! One more word from you, Fletcher, and I'll have you put in a cell!"

Jowls quivering, flecks of froth gathering in the corners of his mouth, the Chief Justice stared at Fletcher with glowering malice, and at length, returned to the matter in hand.

"No, Dr. Prout, I fear you have been deceived. I intend nothing to your discredit, of course, but your transparent goodness of heart has been abused by baser forces, which we shall soon unmask. Pray leave the box."

"As you wish, your Honour." Prout stepped down from the teak and rosewood witness box, and resumed his seat among the Mission personnel.

"Now," resumed the Chief Justice, "We shall get to the heart of the matter in the only way possible, by hearing the facts from the mouth of the accused himself. Let him be called to give his evidence."

When Ajang had been told that he must tell the absolute truth and leave nothing out, and had made it plain through the interpreter that he understood what was expected of him, the Chief Justice, beaming genially, said:

"Now, tell us all you know about that afternoon. Take your time, take your time."

Encouraged by the kindly tones, and realising that this new and terrible *kiap* was for some reason the enemy of Fletcher, Ajang naturally concluded that the red man was looking forward to hearing about his adventures at some length. So he began to describe in luxuriant and rhetorical detail the heat and stillness of that Saturday afternoon, when the whole station drowsed in its siesta, his boredom, his casual glimpse of one of the girls, with bare breasts, washing some clothes in an oil drum cut in half outside her shack. How lust overcame him, how he crept up on her, forced her into the house, and raped her and her two little friends. The third of them was only ten years old, and when she resisted his advances, he struck her in the face with his axe. The torrent of blood drove him into a frenzy, so that he butchered her two companions as well in a flurry of axe blows, which he demonstrated to the court in a pantomime of mindless savagery. Finally, after mutilating them further, he robbed the hut of the few coins he could find and poured paraffin over the bodies and the floor, setting it all alight.

When he had finished this recital, he looked openly and proudly around the court. The Chief Justice was silent for some time, his bewigged head sunk in his hands. Finally, he spoke.

"A cry from the heart, ladies and gentlemen, a cry from the heart, that is what we have heard today. I cannot recall a more melting description of loneliness and despair than that which this man has given us, of his deprivation of female society, his alienation in the strange white man's world of Ungabunga, his cultural shock and bewilderment. Is there one of us here—I mean men, of course— who can swear that, faced with this sudden temptation, he would not have acted *precisely* as did this unfortunate man? Is there?" he roared.

The men of the Mission looked embarrassed, nagged by self-doubt.

"We must ask ourselves, is this unpleasant matter not a judge-ment on us all, are we not all guilty? Did we extend the hand of friendship to our lonely brother, did we take him into our homes, feed him and clothe him? And if we are as much to blame as this wretched man, can we condemn him? No! Compassion and humil-ity, but above all compassion, forbids us to condemn one who has been the victim of countless humiliations and deprivations, like his unfortunate people, for so many years. It is the spirit of the law that gives it life, and that spirit is compassion. The law charges me alone on this island with the functions that a jury normally performs in more privileged quarters of the globe, but I think that I can safely claim to speak for you all when I say that he is Not Guilty."

Ajang, who during this tremendous philippic had begun to fear that the strange *kiap* was disappointed with his story, recovered his spirits as it was translated to him, and by the end was positively bouncing.

"Now, my good fellow," said the Chief Justice, "Is there anything you would like, to compensate you for your ordeal? Anything at all, you have only to ask." He beamed ingratiatingly on the accused.

Ajang, who had not anticipated this turn of events, had to think for a while, but then he brightened, and said:

"I want a shirt."

"Certainly, certainly, a most modest request. Dr. Prout, will you please have a man go to my lodgings and bring the shirt which is drying in the bathroom." Prout despatched a clerk at the double, and in a few minutes he returned carrying a handsome poplin shirt, with thin red stripes. The Chief Justice beckoned Ajang to approach the bench, and arrayed him in the shirt. After playfully offering him a pinch of snuff, which Ajang refused, he dismissed him, telling him to come and see him whenever he liked. Flushed with success, Ajang could not resist prancing down the court before his accusers of the Mission, who tried to look as if they had been on his side all the time. Putting out his tongue at Fletcher and the sergeant, he fled through the door, whooping and yelling, with a handful of his kinsmen who had come down to witness his fate.

"And now," said the Chief Justice, suddenly grim, "We come to the most important business of the day. You, Roger Fletcher, sometime Resident Magistrate of this unhappy island, are charged that on a day between 19— and 19—, you did wilfully murder three men of Niovoro, at that place, the men being Pajok, Mangar, and Rumbek."

Fletcher slowly got up and sauntered over to the dock, where he lounged at his ease. The Chief Justice looked severely at him and asked:

"Do you plead Guilty or Not Guilty?"

"Before I plead anything, I'd like a jury."

"What?"

"You heard. A jury. Any *white* man here is entitled to a jury of four male European residents."

"Could such a law be possible, Mr Moncreif?"

"Yes, Your Honour, it is very clearly the law under the Statutes of Elephant Island."

The only Europeans who met the stringent residence qualifications were Oelrichs, Erny, Smith and Oakley, who were duly sworn amid much good-humoured chaff with the accused that the Chief Justice was unable to quell.

When the disturbance had died down, the Chief Justice said:

"Now, I ask you again, how do you plead?"

"Not Guilty."

The Mission staff were radiant with expectation. At last the brutal ruffian who had terrorised and degraded a whole people was about to receive his just deserts at the hands of the very law which he had so abused. They settled down to their banquet of retribution.

Clearing his throat like a hippopotamus snorting in the swamps, the Chief Justice ordered the principal witness to be summoned to give his evidence. From the back of the court one of the Mission staff went out, and came back in a few minutes leading Snail Slime by the hand. When he was sitting comfortably, the Chief Justice began his examination, with the aid of the interpreter.

"What is your name?"

"Snail Slime."

"I beg your pardon."

"Snail Slime."

"Yes. I see. Well, er, Snail Slime, what village do you come from?"

"Niovoro."

"Were you born there?"

"Yes."

"Have you lived there ever since?"

"Yes."

"So you knew Pajok?"

"Yes, he was my father, my true father."

"What do you mean, your true father?"

"I have many fathers. Pajok begot me on my mother."

"Ah, I see. Now, how old were you when he was killed?"

"I was this high." He indicated a boy of about twelve.

"Do you remember the day well?"

"Yes, very well."

"Tell us about it."

"We had been fighting the Sapo people. We raided them, and burnt their village, and killed many of their pigs, yes, very many of their pigs and had many of their women."

"But you were only a little boy."

"Yes. I stayed at home, I was small, but we all knew. All my fathers went to Sapo, to burn it and kill the pigs and have the women, and we killed a man and his wife in their garden, and chopped them into pieces, into very small pieces."

"Yes, yes, and what happened then?

"Mr Fletcher heard, and he was very angry, and he came with the police to Niovoro, and killed many pigs, and burnt the houses, and the women were crying because of the pigs, and the police took the knives that are on the end of their guns, and heated them in the fire, so that they became as red as the *tavala* flower, and we were all afraid."

"Yes, go on."

"And Mr. Fletcher told us to make a line, all of us who were big, big enough to kill. And the police hit us with pieces of wood, on our backsides, because we were afraid, and did not want to make the line."

"But why did you have to stand in the line?"

"I did not have to go in the line. I told you, I was too small."

The Judge looked slightly baffled, but pressed on:

"What happened then?"

"We made the line, and the police took their gun knives from the fire, and they were very hot, and Mr. Fletcher said we must lick the knives."

"You mean, he told the men in the line to lick the knives?"

"Yes, that is what I just told you. And he said, 'You who killed the man and woman at Sapo, and chopped them into little pieces, your tongues will curl up like leaves in the flames, and they will swell and choke you, and you will die, but the men who did not kill them, you will feel nothing, not even pain.' And all the men licked the knives, and some men felt no pain, but my true father, and Mangar his brother, and his cousin Rumbek, they all cried out, and fell on the ground, and the blood came out of their mouths, and they were very sick. And Mr Fletcher, he said they were bad man, and they would die. He came and stood over them, and made them look into his eyes, and they were the eyes of death. He cursed them, and said that when the sun came up they would be dead. And it was as he said. My fathers, all my fathers, were dead when the sun came up. And they cried all night, and were very sick, and our women were crying and they brought water, but they could not drink, because their tongues swelled up. That is all my talk. I talk true."

The Chief Justice glared at Fletcher from under knotted brows, and if his *pince-nez* had been burning-glasses Fletcher would have been utterly consumed.

"Well, you have heard this man's evidence, which as a narrative of terror and the degradation of one's fellow human beings eclipses anything I have ever heard in thirty years in the courts. Can you deny it? Can you deny that you caused these men's deaths by inflicting such terrible burns on their tongues that they shortly after died of the effects—or do we need to call more witnesses?"

"Yeah, well, this kanaka's had it in for me since I took a swipe at 'im a year back."

"Are you confessing to further acts of brutality?"

"I'm just sayin' that he's got a motive for tryin' to blacken me reputation."

There was a flutter of laughter in the court, and even the Judge permitted himself a smile.

"Well, Fletcher, I'm sure we're very concerned about your reputation, hence the present proceedings. Now perhaps you'll come to the point, and tell us if you can find any fault with his evidence."

"No, not as far as it goes…"

"As far as it goes?" erupted the Chief Justice. "By God, Sir, it goes far enough to hang you… or… or… at least imprison you for life!" He fell back panting, his face liver-colored and sweating, and taking out a great horn snuff box he indulged furiously, until his whole body was convulsed with sneezes.

"When yer've finished blowin' yer hooter, may be ye'll let me get a word in. Everythin' that little shit said is true, for once, except that those three blokes didn't die from lickin' the bayonets."

"What did they die of, then?"

"My curse."

This time there was a roar of outraged laughter, and much exchange of sniggering comments among the Mission staff.

"You pitiful wretch. If ever there was proof of the saying that all power corrupts you see it before you in the dock. Look at him, look at him, drunk with power, crazed with the most deluded superstitions of those he ruled. It's a tale out of Bedlam, a warning to us all."

"So what you're sayin, Judge, is that those three blokes died of physical injuries, inflicted under my orders?"

"Of course that is what I am saying."

"Just let me get one thing straight. If I could prove that I killed 'em by my curse, just for argument's sake, would I be guilty of murder?"

"I really do not see the point of this line of questioning at all"

"Perhaps I can elucidate it, your Honour," said Moncreif. "What the accused means is that according to Section 37 of the Statutes of Elephant Island it is deemed impossible for any person to cause the death or illness of another 'by witchcraft, magic, or other pretended necromantic arts.' Therefore if, hypothetically, a person were in fact to bring about the death of another by such means, he could not be charged with murder."

"I see," said Robinson, with some astonishment.

Fletcher got up from the dock and walked over to Snail Slime, who was still sitting in the witness box, and fixed him with a deadly stare. The native's eyes dropped, but Fletcher's unwavering gaze forced him to raise them again, and he sat staring at Fletcher, transfixed. Fletcher reached into his pocket and brought out a pointed splinter of bone, dirty and yellowed; violently, he stabbed at Snail Slime's face, and hissed:

"By the power of the bone, may thy bowels be knotted.

"By the power of the bone, may thy bladder be ruptured.

"By the power of the bone, may thy blood turn to pus.

"By the power of the bone, may thy windpipe be clogged.

"By the power of the bone, may thy body swell up, and fester, and die"

Snail Slime seemed to crumple under the malefic blast and, clutching his throat, he staggered from the witness box, making gargling noises, and tottered across the court, seeing nothing. As he approached the Judge's Bench his legs swerved under him and he fell heavily, his limbs twitching spasmodically. Smith ran forward and bent over the plainly dying man, and after listening to his heart beat and taking his pulse he looked up at the Chief Justice.

"I know such cases, sir, they are hopeless. It is psychosomatic influence, of course, but the natives' belief is so strong that unless the spell is taken away the man will die in a few hours."

Fletcher had gone back to the dock, where he sat watching the proceedings with grim amusement. Robinson stumbled down from his seat, and tried ineffectually to rouse the victim by fanning his face. Prout joined him and wanted to apply artificial respiration, but was restrained by Smith.

"In such cases, the only hope is for the man who places the spell to make more magic to take it away, and then the victim will recover. Roger, you have your demonstration, do you want this man to die? Please, I beg of you, do not kill him!"

"Sorry, Smithy, the bastard's gotta die. I have to prove I can kill by sorcery, like I killed those three at Niovoro."

"I agree with the Doctor, Mr Fletcher," said Robinson, "The man is plainly dying."

"Yes," Prout added his own fervent appeal. "You can't kill this wretched man in cold blood. I implore you, release him before he dies!"

"But unless he does die, I haven't proved me point, and yer can still get me for murder."

"But this *is* murder," cried Prout.

"Blood oath, it ain't. As Mike there said, if you can find anything in the Statutes of Elephant Island to say that a bloke can kill another by magic, sorcery, or any other means than violence or poison, I'm a dead dingo's donger. The old timers wanted to teach the natives that magic and suchlike was all bullshit, kanaka superstition, so the Statutes say it's impossible to kill anyone by it. O'course, there's Section 38, dealin' with those who *pretend* to be able to cast spells, causing great fear thereby among the native people, carries a thirty-bob fine, or four months' hard labour, or both, but I'm not bloody well pretendin', as yer can see, so yer can't even get me under Section 38."

Snail Slime was now in a coma, breathing stertorously.

"You intellectuals think yer know all the answers, with yer books and yer long words. Well, yer know bugger-all. I tried to tell Prout when he first came that there was more to runnin' this place than met the eye, but he wouldn't listen. Charlie Bryanston, the RM before me, tried to do everythin' legal and proper. Used to chase some murderin' bastards round the mountains for a few weeks, bring 'em back to the nick, and then tell 'em they didn't have to answer any questions they didn't want to, and had a right to plead Not Guilty. The kanakas thought he was off his flamin' rocker. Dead right. When yer dealing with these jokers yer got to use the methods they understand. So when I found they thought I was one of their old gods come back to earth, I had it made. Used the police to bash 'em if they got stroppy, and the real hard cases I knocked off meself. O'course, I could've shot 'em, or slung 'em over a cliff, but in this day and age I couldn't take the chance of some legal bastard comin' snufflin' around, like Prout when he first showed up. Didn't take him long to

figure out there must've been killin's, and ask why there was nothin'
in the station books. But I knew I was clear as long as I used magic.
The police bumped off a few, but that was self-defence, under attack.
You can't get anyone for that. Allowed under the Statutes."

The Chief Justice returned slowly to the bench, a very sober man.
The eyes of the Mission were still riveted on the dying Snail Slime,
and the sight removed any temptation to snigger. Smith had him
placed on a stretcher and carried over to the dispensary. When the
stretcher party had left, the Chief Justice addressed the court.

"This is the most astonishing case I have ever known. I'm sick-
ened and shocked by what has happened today. But Mr. Fletcher is
legally correct. If the laws of Elephant Island deem it impossible to
kill by witchcraft or similar means, and I have now verified that they
do, then a man cannot be charged with so doing. And in the case
of the deaths of the three men at Niovoro, it has not been proved
beyond reasonable doubt that they died as the result of the injuries
inflicted upon them. A charge of assault clearly lies against the accused for subjecting them to the ordeal in the first place, but since
the men are long dead it is no longer possible to establish how grave
those injuries were, and to what extent they were produced by an
exercise of Mr Fletcher's powers which are deemed not to exist, for
legal purposes. I have no alternative, therefore, but to direct the jury
to acquit the accused."

Robinson rose and left the Bench by the Judge's door behind,
head bowed, without another word. His departure went unnoticed,
as the jury let out a great yell of triumph, in which they were joined
by the police, who had packed the court as Fletcher's trial began.
Fletcher was carried out shoulder-high, to the accompaniment of
showers of ribald insults directed at the Mission. That night there
was a mighty celebration piss-up at the Cosmopolitan, and Snail

Slime died in the early hours of the morning without regaining consciousness.

Chapter XIV

IN THE WEEK BEFORE Bastille Day on Elephant Island, various well-wishers flew in and out of Ungabunga, a sprinkling of academics, administrators, politicians, and those hoping to sell some of the necessities of life to the soon-to-be independent Republic. The staff of the Mission had been toiling through the mountains to spread the news of the Independence celebrations on Bastille Day; the native people received the invitation with polite interest, said they would be very pleased to come, and went on with the work in their new gardens.

A full programme was arranged for the visitors, and tours of the Gas Works, the Palace of Justice, and the House of Assembly were fully booked. Some hardy souls even ventured into the mountains, where Schultz was supervising the construction of prefabricated village halls in a few selected villages, to which women as well as men would be admitted. This was the inspiration of Phyllis Prout, who had been determined to abolish the sexist privileges of the men's houses as soon as she learnt of their existence, in which she was strongly supported by Rebeccah Bloom. By the judicious sale of soft drinks it was intended to lure the men into the company of their womenfolk for evenings of harmless mutual conviviality, thus rendering the men's houses obsolete within a short period of time.

The Moroks had been delighted by these new buildings, since the walls had large areas of glass-louvred windows; at first, misled by their hardness, they had thought that the windows were as tough as metal, but a few careless incidents revealed that they were eminently breakable, and they discovered that they quite liked the sound of smashing glass. But the large area of window made the new village halls much colder than the traditional men's houses, so gas fires as well as stoves had been installed, fed from cylinders of propane filled at the Ungabunga Gas Works. All the prefabricated sections of the new halls, like the cylinders, were airlifted into the villages by helicopters, which were also available to spare the visitors the unaccustomed rigours of walking. After an exhilarating hour's tour of their selected village, where they were greatly impressed by the cleanness and enthusiasm for sanitation demonstrated by the villagers, they were treated to stale buns and lukewarm orangeade in the village hall, and sent on their way by a delegation of notables dressed in their new garments from Erny's store.

The Mission had also gone ahead to install microwave repeater stations on the main peaks to ensure that the people were brought fully into the family of nations by finally being able to receive television and make international phone calls. The visitors were vastly impressed by these and all the other revolutionary improvements in the Moroks' way of life, and it was generally agreed that the whole project was a triumph of enlightened aid, so much so that Prout became almost weary of modestly fending off the showers of congratulations.

Lord Southall's Learjet arrived a few days before the 14th. The great man had been a trifle put out on the journey by his travelling companions, since he had given a free passage from Port Moresby to the delegate from New Patagonia who, it turned out, thought he was God and refused to speak to anyone, and also to an American representative of Justice Inc., Wayne T. Ruger, who had a large square face, artificially greyed hair, and cultivated the air of a judge, with spectacles, silver tie and dark suit. In offering him a lift, Southall had supposed that he represented a firm of legal publishers, or some such. It was only when the aircraft was passing over the Huon Gulf that Ruger clarified his job:

"No sir, my firm is more concerned with the practical aspects of the judicial process."

"Really? You mean Amnesty International, that sort of thing?"

"I can't say we've had any dealings with them. We're really interested in supplying the needs of the developing nations which have problems maintaining law and order."

"Oh."

"Yeah, we have a number of specialised departments: surveillance consultation, security equipment installation, supply of training teams for guard-dog patrols, and so on, and so on. Put it this way, if it's good for the rule of law, it's good for Justice Incorporated."

"And which department do you represent?"

"I have the good fortune to head up the Department of Community Protection."

"Protection against what, if I may ask?"

"Saboteurs, traitors, skyjackers, perverts, anti-social forces of the most dangerous sort."

"Do you mean that you build prisons?" asked Southall, with a hint of distaste.

"No sir, I specialise in elimination equipment. Gas chambers, guillotines, electric chairs, humane killers, you name it, we sell it, and if we don't sell it, we custom build it to the client's personal order."

"Good God!"

"Yeah, just got in from Amnesia this morning. These guys may be only just out of the Stone Age, but when it comes to modern technology they're front runners all the way. Showed their new President a film clip of our latest electric chair—disposes of the body by microwave incineration, all solid-state circuitry, very important in tropical climates—and he slapped an order for twenty right there in my hand. Not like those Catatonian crumbs. Goddam stick-in-the-mud traditionalists. Been having some problems of civil insurrection, and called me in. All I got was an order for ten lousy hydraulic garrotting chairs. That's a blacksmith's job if ever I saw one. I warned 'em we'd had trouble with the neck-snapping linkage where it passes through the post, and would they listen? No, of course not. It's that olde worlde Spanish tradition."

"If you don't mind, I think I feel rather ill." Lord Southall rose and went into his private state room, where his valet gave him a large brandy and put him to bed for the rest of the flight.

While Southall was being fêted by an obsequious Mission, Fletcher was on a lone patrol in the mountains. He had felt for some time that since cleanliness was as foreign to the Morok character as godliness, their sudden enthusiasm for latrines could not be taken at its face value. But all his questions, hints, and insinuations had been deftly turned aside; the Houses of Filth were "nothing," "the commands of the Father of Nyikang," "they hide our filth in the fashion of the red men," and so on. In fact, the Moroks were afraid that Fletcher, in his strictness, would take away their riches when they finally blossomed, and the word had gone out that the two Revelations were to be hidden from him.

He intended staying the night at Lavalava, and had gone out for a stroll down to the gardens in the evening, after the women had left them for the day. The sunset that evening was reflected from banks of cloud to the east, and lit up the landscape in a brilliant purple glow that revealed every leaf and stone with unearthly clarity. Leaning over a fence that surrounded a mature yam garden, his eye was caught by a glint of orange in the soil. He climbed over and picked his way to the spot through the sticks supporting the vines of the yams. Scraping away the soil, he uncovered a fire-engine from the Chicago Fire Department, clogged with earth, and its paint soft and peeling with damp. His interest thoroughly aroused, he cast about, and soon discovered a whole crop of similar toys. He took a sheet of newspaper from his pocket and rolled himself a cigarette, and walked back from the garden deep in thought.

On the way he fell in with young Dayim, an amiable fellow by Morok standards, who was carrying a bunch of bananas home from his trees down by the river. Fletcher examined them appreciatively.

"The men of Lavalava are powerful gardeners."

"Aye, Tikame, thou speakest truth; our hands give life to every living thing."

"'Tis not your hands alone, man. 'Tis the words of power that ye above all men know."

"Aye, Tikame, in all the Tolava valley there are none to compare with the men of Lavalava, for sowing, or for blighting."

"'Tis a fair crop of the red men's playthings that ye raise in this season." Dayim looked startled, and Fletcher continued. "If this crop ripeneth, ye will have more of these good things than the red men themselves."

He was still not sure exactly what the Moroks expected to happen, but Dayim was by now persuaded that Fletcher knew all, and that for him the two revelations were casual knowledge.

As they rested under an evergreen oak, relaxing on the crisp dry carpet of dead leaves, Fletcher gave him tobacco and paper, and in half an hour had elicited the whole story, of the dream of Abuk, and the triumph which it had brought to Lavalava and the whole of the

Tolava valley by frustrating the braggarts of Laripa and the Loma. However, even accustomed as he was to the tortuous reasoning of the Moroks, Fletcher was staggered by the theory behind the Houses of Filth, and was hard-pressed not to burst out laughing. But in the deepening twilight his facial struggles passed unnoticed, and at length, their cigarettes finished, they parted company.

From the verandah of the rest house, Fletcher looked down the Tolava valley to Ungabunga. The station itself was hidden behind a spur of Mount Browning, but the thousands of fairy lights hung up for the celebration of Independence Day radiated a perceptible glow up into the surrounding dusk. Some village women brought him roasted sweet potatoes and pork, and a bamboo tube of water to make tea, and as he ate he brooded on the Mission.

What did they know of his great mountains, their crests smoking with mist and rain, gashed with cataracts and foaming torrents; of the troll-haunted forests whose vast, dim, silences were broken only by the shrieks of birds of paradise, and the crash of hunter and hunted; and of the Moroks, his own wild people, chanting, smashing, lusting in the ancient world of their ancestors? Was all this to be made tidy and safe, a nice place to bring the wife and kiddies on a package tour? All to be choked and constipated with paper, conferences and committees, inspections and minutes and reports and the eternal clack of typewriters and intellectual tongues?

Just below the rest house, the new village hall loomed as a dull white shape. Its interior was already sordid with scraps of food and broken glass from the louvres. If the Mission had its way, this ancient unfathomable land would be tamed to a tropical slum, and its inhabitants rendered as impotent as barnyard fowls, but now, at last, he'd got them where he wanted them. As soon as he proved to the Moroks that they had been deceived, they would fall upon the Mission like dogs on rabbits. He felt like a man on the cliffs above some frivolous holiday resort, packed with mindless revellers, about to lever a great boulder from its bed and send it tossing and crashing down the scree, to stir a grinding avalanche in its wake, that would obliterate his enemies in a roaring chaos of dust and screams.

On Friday afternoon Ungabunga awaited the arrival of the People. For their convenience marquees had been erected on the airstrip in which they could spend the night, and be refreshed and relaxed for the great events of Saturday. The Day itself was to begin with a tableau depicting racial harmony, presented by the expatriate and indigenous children of the station, with much exchanging of garlands and what passed for Greek dancing under the supervision of Noreen Hiscock. After a buffet lunch, and a speech by Lord Southall, the People were to ratify the new Constitution by acclamation, and the Mission, the visitors, and their indigenous hosts would then partake of a traditional supper of roast pork and sweet-potatoes, while for those interested in exploring the rich variety of local cuisine there would be frogs boiled in bamboo tubes, wallabies baked in their skins, and pregnant cane-rats on sticks. Sunday was to be devoted to inter-racial, non-competitive sports, such as blind-man's bluff and grandmother's footsteps, games which everyone could win, and all could claim prizes.

As Friday afternoon wore on, many eyes scanned the two tracks leading down to the station, looking expectantly for the first glimpse of the Moroks. Just after three, two horsemen were spotted, rounding the last spur of the track from Niovoro, and when they arrived Fletcher and Oakley were eagerly questioned.

"Nuthin' doin' that we could see. Just a few maries on the road," and they rode off to the pub.

At tea-time Southall, who was staying in the Presidential Palace, expressed his misgivings to Prout.

"Are you sure they know what day it is? After all, they don't have calendars."

"I rather doubt if it was that. Our staff made it very clear to the chiefs, and they're highly intelligent men."

"I see. Well, could you have offended them in some way?"

"Oh no, I don't think that could be the trouble. You're probably right. Some ridiculous misunderstanding. Even with the use of Neo-Melanesian, we've never beaten the language problem entirely."

"Neo-Melanesian? What's that?"

"It's the correct name for Pidgin English, as the old plantation-owners and those sorts of people called it. Anyway, we can communicate quite well with it, but misunderstandings still occur, mainly with technological words."

They were interrupted by the sound of a helicopter, and Prout went over to the window in time to see a red Alouette disappearing behind the House of Assembly in a cloud of dust. The United Nations escort ship *Dove*, on its way to Nouméa for a good will visit, had anchored in Byron Bay that afternoon and radioed its arrival to the Mission. There was to be a dinner in honour of Southall that night, so an invitation had been sent immediately to the captain and his officers, who had presumably now arrived.

Moia and Madame Negretti had spent a daemonic afternoon slaving and hurling abuse at one another in their steam-filled kitchen, sometimes breaking out in mutual exchanges of flying toast-racks and saucepans, but eventually, in a lather of sweat and execrations, the great dinner for the most important guests was prepared.

But before they could be allowed to quench their belly-rumblings, the niceties of Culture decreed that they should endure an hour of chamber music, performed not for Southall, who was tone-deaf, but purely in honour of the occasion. The programme had advanced to a work by one of the more deranged of the Central European atonalists when the sounds of discordant singing and smashing glass slowly detached themselves from the music and heralded the arrival of Fletcher, disgustingly drunk, supported by Oelrichs and Moncreif, and coming to spoil the party.

The cellist was struggling with a recalcitrant solo passage, but from the agony of the sounds he was producing, he might just as well have had a pig between his legs and been castrating it. Fletcher observed in hoarse, but penetrating, tones that if that was supposed to be music he'd show them what sort of tune *he* could produce with a bow up the bloody fiddler's orifice. The crudity of this suggestion brought a sudden silence over the gathering, disturbed only by Fletcher rummaging noisily among the dishes on the table. To ease the tension, Madame Negretti gesticulated to the quartet to get back on the job, and as they rapidly selected a more melodious diversion, she began introducing Fletcher to some of the bystanders one of whom, short, assured, glacial of manner and spectacled, evidently a journalist of progressive opinions, had pointedly ignored Fletcher's intrusion.

"Ah, Mr. Crispin, you must meet Roger Fletcher, our Warden of the Goldfields."

"Roger *who*, of *where*?"

"Are you bloody deaf? I'm Roger Fletcher, of never mind where." Fletcher peered at Crispin more closely, and then fingered his collar.

"Is that dandruff, or 've yer been out in the snow?" He seized Crispin's slender neck in a genial grasp. "Now I'll bet there's something yer don't know about the kanakas on this island, eh," and he shook Crispin vigorously.

"What's that?" quavered the journalist of advanced opinions.

"They won't stand for bloody dandruff, and that's the truth. Only one cure for it."

A large bowl of yellow custard caught his eye. "What's that yer got there, Angelina?" Without waiting for a reply, he dipped both hands into the custard and began plastering it well into Crispin's chestnut curls, at the same time explaining affably to a large lady next to him, who looked like a Russian discus thrower and who was watching, transfixed.

"Now, when yer get inter bed tonight break a coupl 'a eggs on his head and rub well into the scalp, see?" He was interrupted by the protesting discus thrower.

"We not married."

"Never mind that. We're all broad-minded here. The main thing is to rub the eggs well in before the eggs set."

"He never come into my bed!"

"Well, when yer on the floor, or wherever yer do it, don't forget the eggs, then in the morning it'll all 'ave set nicely, then yer take a sharp axe and chop it off, and with a bit of luck yer'll chop the bastard's head off too! Ha! Ha! Ha!" He released the wretched Crispin, who, blinded with custard, stumbled over a chair and fell blubbering in rage and humiliation on the floor.

Madame Negretti had lived at Ungabunga long enough to take such pleasantries as a matter of course, but the guests had led more sheltered lives and either quailed, swelled with outraged dignity, or prepared to do violence to Fletcher. A man of the last category was Major Larsen, the officer in charge of the Dove's helicopter: he was small, immaculate, and with a pair of malignant green eyes which glared indignantly at Fletcher and Oelrichs.

Madame Negretti, realising that the musical evening had been conclusively ended by Fletcher and that things were rapidly getting out of hand, authoritatively announced that dinner was served, and set about laying extra places for the unexpected guests.

"Well, my Lord," said Oelrichs, in between mouthfuls of paté. "Are you satisfied with the Mission's accomplishments so far?"

"There's no need to call me 'My Lord'," said Southall, stiffly, "That kind of thing is rather out nowadays. But I'm very pleased indeed by what I've seen. Dr. Prout and the Mission deserve every credit."

"And do you think the people will live up to expectations?"

"Well, of course. We've shown them the benefits of civilized life, you don't imagine they'll turn their backs on them now, do you?"

"Don't you feel that it might have been a good idea to teach them to read first?"

Southall was becoming restive under this cross-examination, and said, brusquely:

"No, I don't. All recent research has shown that education is really about learning to live together in a community, developing tolerance and understanding, and this is the true basis for a civilized society. Book learning is all very well, but it's tainted with élitism, and I'm afraid that it's too often been a specious excuse for prolonging colonial rule."

He turned his attention pointedly to his neighbour on his left, filling her glass.

"I did not hear your name distinctly," said Larsen. " 'Ollis', did you say it was?"

"Oelrichs, Oelrichs, old chap, but I'm English in spite of it."

"So. And your friend, what is his name?"

"Ah, Major," interrupted Prout, beaming with tipsy malice. "We're honoured by the presence of Mr. Roger Fletcher, Roaring Roger to his friends, I believe. Late ruler of this island, and still Warden of the Goldfields."

"Ruler, you say, Dr. Prout? Is this the man who has defied United Nations authority for so long?"

"What?" Fletcher looked up from a turkey carcase, shreds of meat dangling from his lips and beard, "What's that you said?"

"I said," repeated Larsen, "that you are the man who has defied the authority of the United Nations."

"Too bloody right, I have. I've been waiting a year for you dozy bastards to fall arse over tip, and tonight's the night. 'Aven't you lot been wonderin' where all yer brown brothers 've got to, eh? Should've been swarmin' in like wasps round a jam jar!"

He reached out for a bottle of burgundy and took a long swig. Prout frowned, and shook his head.

"There's just been a slight misunderstanding over dates. We'll soon have everything straightened out."

"More than a slight misunderstanding, mate, and it's you lot that's going to be straightened out. Flattened out, more like! Do yer know why they 'aven't come? I'll tell yer. There's been a ruddy great cargo cult roarin' away in the mountains the last six or eight months, right under yer noses, and that's the only reason they 'aven't slung yer all out on yer arses already."

"Rubbish! Rubbish!" responded a chorus of voices.

"And who started it all off? That twerp Daubeny. The bloke who gave 'em man-traps to catch their supper. 'The cannibals' friend'… jeez! Anyhow, they were tryin' to figure out why Prout wanted 'em to build shit 'ouses, see, when up comes Tristram, like the young genius he is, and as good as tells 'em that crap turns into money and goodies, if yer know what ter do with it. They put two and two together and made seventeen, like they usually bloody do, and next thing they're beaverin' away diggin' a set o' thunder boxes yer could drop the *Queen Mary* down and bustin' their guts tryin' to fill 'em. It was those mugs at Laripa that got the bright idea. They're all up there now, lyin' awake like kids at Christmas, waitin' to see what Santa's bringin' them. Sun up tomorrer, they'll be down those 'oles like flamin' ferrets to dig up the loot. And by Christ, if they don't find it, they're gonna be down 'ere askin' you lot some very nasty questions!"

He grinned at them with ferocious glee.

"Absolute piffle," sniffed Prout. "How do you know all this, unless you've been stirring them up?"

"I been kicking around up there the last week or so. Turned up another cargo cult at Lavalava. They got pissed off with Laripa runnin' the show and wanted to do their own thing. So they got the bright idea that the toys in Erny's store were some kind o' seed, and if yer planted 'em with the right spells they'd grow inter bloody full-sized Cadillacs and steam-rollers, and God knows what else. And they'll be goin' crook tomorrer mornin' too."

"For my part," said Southall, "I have the utmost confidence in Dr Prout's judgment. Must we listen to any more of these illiterate ravings?"

Fletcher rose in his chair, dribbling burgundy into his beard, plainly meditating some atrocity against the Guest of Honour, when Prout diverted his attention.

"What's all this got to do with our celebrations? I don't see any connection at all."

"There's a bloody good connection, as they see it. Yer've been tellin' 'em that come tomorrer all their troubles are over, it's goin' to be a new world, like all their birthdays've come at once, and all that bullshit, so they reckon yer must've meant that it's the day when the goodies arrive."

That was true, so far as it went, but it wasn't the whole truth. Fletcher had also told the Moroks that Prout intended to betray them, and that come the promised day, they would find nothing in their Houses of Filth.

The rest of his remarks were drowned in noisy abuse and general uproar. Prout leaned over and shouted in Fletcher's ear.

"I don't believe a word of this. It's just a vicious lie to upset the Mission in the hour of its success."

"It's nothin' to do with me, mate. Yer lot got yerselves inter this. Yer buggered up the fort, the gaol, the police, so the place is fallin' apart. Yer can put it back together tomorrer mornin'. When it comes to the crunch, yer'll find a fort's a bloody sight more use than a gas works."

He got up and wandered round the table in search of more wine, while the babble of angry voices raged around him. Collaring a bottle of port, he tore the leg off a goose and munched at it for a few minutes, washing it down with long gulps from the bottle. His eyes wandered hazily over the assembled guests, until they fastened on a strikingly lovely girl, with long black hair and pneumatic bosom, in a dress that was both scarlet and revealing. Leaning over the table he extended a greasy hand to her.

"I didn't get yer name. I'm Roger Fletcher. Enjoyin' yerself?"

"It's hardly what I expected," she replied, coolly, "But I suppose it'll be a good story for my grandchildren one day." Fletcher's eyes were riveted on the heaving globes of her bosom, and his face split in a lecherous grin.

"You're the first decent lookin' sheila in Ungabunga for donkey's years. How about stayin' on?"

"Staying on? If you're right about tomorow there won't be much to stay on for, will there? Anyway, I have to leave with Daddy in a couple of days."

"With who?"

"My father. Lord Southall."

"Shit. Is *he* yer old man?"

"Yes. And I don't like the way you talk about him."

Fletcher lay across the table, leering at her, sweat streaming down his face.

"I wasn't talking about him. I was talking about yer."

"Well, why don't we talk about you instead? I can see why they call you Roaring Roger, anyway."

"No yer flamin' well can't. At least, not while I've still got me strides on."

He clambered fully on to the table and stood there, swaying and stumbling among the dishes in his muddy riding boots, with wine and food splattered down his khaki shirt. Waving his bottle he bellowed at the horrified crowd.

"They call me Roaring Roger because I go to bed with a Rooaaring Roger! And I wake up in the night with a Rooaaring Roger! And I get up in the morning with a Rooaaring Roger! Put me to stud! I can breed!"

Then he collapsed unconscious among the plates and tureens.

Chapter XV

A S FLETCHER HAD PREDICTED, the Moroks spent a restless, expectant night awaiting the dawn, and voices continued to murmur spasmodically in the huts and men's houses throughout the mountains until the sky started to lighten, around six o'clock. As dawn arrived, smoke began to filter out from under the thatch of the huts, as the fires were blown to life, but everyone's excitement was too great to think of eating.

At Laripa, Malek marshalled his warriors for a ceremonial procession to the House of Filth, and as they donned their tall headdresses of paradise plumes, he consulted with Garang on the auspicious moment to unveil their riches.

"When the sun striketh the Peaks of Karama, then shall all be revealed," declared Garang with an air of authority. At about half-past six the warriors were ready, their women clustering at the rear, all carrying several capacious string bags to bear away the wealth that would shortly be theirs, laughing and chattering. Even Nyikang had found the strength to crawl from the men's house, and tottered beside the resplendent fighting men, as with shout and song they began their procession.

Arriving at the House of Filth, on Malek's signal, they began demolishing it with axes, in wild enthusiasm. When the posts and beams were all cast down, and strewn around the hole, Malek forgot the speech he had intended making, so great was the general fever, and he also forgot his dignity as a chief, and joined in the removal of the timbers over the hole. The smell which arose from it was not reassuring. Malek struck a heroic posture at the edge of the pit, as his supporters fastened him into a crudely improvised harness.

"I go now, to fetch you tidings of the red men's treasure."

Four strong men began to lower their chief into the stinking gloom of the latrine. The men had to stand back to avoid being dragged in themselves, so the only indications of his progress were the thuds and periodic falls of earth as Malek descended. Suddenly, a clamour of muffled shrieks and yells broke the tense silence, and the men began to haul Malek up. Twenty seconds' grunting exertion dragged him back to the light of day, and the audience fell back as their filthy, dripping, malodorous leader sprawled over the edge of the hole, weeping with shock and mortification.

"Aaaaahh! Ekeh! Ekeh!" breathed the crowd, in growing shock and horror. Garang quickly seized the initiative. Breaking his staff over his thigh, he shrieked:

"Betrayed! Betrayed! Tikame spoke truth indeed. We are deceived. The red men have lied!"

"By my mother's bones, we shall take mighty vengeance," roared Malek, wiping at himself ineffectually. "To arms, to arms!"

In every village the same scene was being repeated, almost simultaneously, and the valleys resounded to the long drawn cries of rage, as village called to village its dismal tale of humiliated expectations. In a couple of hours, after some notably uncharitable speeches given by the chiefs at the expense of the Mission, all the warriors had discarded their ceremonial feathers, and assuming their war plumage of black and scarlet around their brows, began silently padding toward their enemies, their minds filled with visions of blood and destruction.

At Lavalava, Abuk and his men, distraught with grief and disappointment, had cast aside the corroded, peeling toys with petulant fury and, eyes glowing under heavy brows, took up their weapons, their clubs, their quivering spears, their massive black-palm bows, and came down like a torrent along the track, crouching and hissing in their traditional war dance.

The sunrise that had brought humiliation and despair to the Moroks was, for Prout, the Dawn of Reason on his very own day, Bastille Day, the final liberation of Elephant Island from its long night of superstition and the tyranny of the past. He and Phyllis were up early, and after a nutritious breakfast to sustain them for the challenging day ahead, went down to Hut 27 where a special meeting of the Bastille Day Committee had been convened. Tristram had slept badly, worried by the absence of the people and by Fletcher's claims at dinner the previous night, and as soon as Prout arrived he burst out:

"Surely, Dr. Prout, we ought to do something to check up about this story of a cargo-cult?"

"I'm really surprised, Tristram, that you should have taken Fletcher's outburst quite so seriously. The man was soused. It was pure mischief-making. The only remarkable thing is that the illiterate oaf had ever heard of cargo-cults—probably got it from Oelrichs—but we must never underestimate the extraordinary cunning of the uneducated. It was nothing more than a prank intended to disconcert us in the hour of our triumph," he said, with a reassuring smile.

The rest of the committee loudly agreed, and Prout went on.

"Fletcher is just an absurd reactionary who can't accept that his little conservative world is collapsing about his ears, doomed by the progressive forces of history. I have absolutely no doubt that everything we have worked so hard for is falling into place, and that by the end of today, we shall feel dizzy with success. But there are still some events in the programme that we need to sort out, and since the people aren't here yet, we shall have time to discuss them."

He was referring to such problems as the recent demand by Rebeccah Bloom, as Secretary of Political Consciousness, that there should be a *tableau vivant* representing the defeat of colonialism by the oppressed peoples of the world, which clashed in the timetable with Noreen Hiscock's Greek dancing and had sparked a vicious dispute between the two ladies. This, and other matters, required Prout's urgent attention before the ceremonies could begin. Lord Southall was a silent but increasingly impatient observer of the proceedings as they droned on. He, too, had been reflecting on Fletcher's remarks of the night before, and by eight o'clock he finally intervened.

"It would ease my mind considerably if we could at least find out where the people are, and what they are doing."

"But of course," replied Prout, looking up briefly from his paperwork, and rather relieved to be rid of Southall's brooding presence. "It might be quickest if you asked Major Larsen to take you in the helicopter."

Southall lost no time in finding the major, and a short time later they took off. Larsen swung the chopper low over the terrain, coming over the crests of the ridges at a hundred feet so that it could not be heard until it was directly overhead. As they flew up the gorge of the Limilimi, they came upon the Laripa warriors striding out for Ungabunga, all armed to the teeth. The Moroks stopped, startled by the helicopter that seemed to come from nowhere, but when Larsen banked in a tight turn for a second pass they loosed a ragged shower of arrows and one or two spears that fell hopelessly short. Larsen quickly gained some height and set a course to take them further up the valley. As he did so Southall shouted at him.

"It seems that Fletcher was right after all." Larsen nodded, and with Southall's permission radioed the station with the appalling news. Reception was poor in the gorges, however, so the transmission was brief. They flew on across the valley, and found another ferocious contingent pouring down the track from Niovoro, and at the sight of those furious faces, gibbering with rage, Larsen peeled away and swung the chopper back down towards Ungabunga.

The news of the advancing Moroks had spread quickly around the station, but while some felt the icy hand of terror, most of the Mission, secure in their record of selfless achievement for the good of the people and in their confidence in Dr. Prout, treated the news simply as an interesting subject of speculation. Nevertheless, as the whine and clatter of the returning Alouette echoed around the strip, a small crowd clustered around to hear what Lord Southall had to say. The great man was, in a strange way, rather enjoying the situation as a challenge to his powers, and, standing in the doorway of the helicopter, he made a short but forceful speech on the urgency of the situation. It was designed to stiffen sinews rather than to create panic and encouraged them to wait for further instructions. Here he seriously overestimated the proportion of sinew to jelly in the moral fibre of his audience, but unaware of this, he made his way with Larsen to Hut 27.

The meeting had heard the return of the helicopter, so they all looked up expectantly as Southall and Larsen came in.

"I imagine they will be here soon, as I told you," said Prout, with a smile.

"They will," replied Southall grimly, "but certainly not to join in the festivities of Independence Day. It appears that Fletcher was quite right and that they are coming in force to attack us."

"Rubbish," replied Prout, in tones of complete indifference. "I have never heard such nonsense. What can have put such an idea into your heads?"

"It was clear as daylight," replied Southall. "They were large war-parties bristling with weapons, they fired arrows and threw spears at us, and were obviously hostile. Extremely hostile." Larsen nooded in agreement.

"With all due respect," said Prout, looking at them over his reading glasses, "I think my knowledge of Morok culture and traditions is rather greater than either of yours. When attending great festivities it is their custom to come heavily armed, and displays of aggression of the type that you witnessed are required by Morok etiquette from the guests towards their hosts. You have simply misinterpreted local culture in an alarmist fashion."

"But if you would only come and look for yourself–" broke in Larsen:

"I have no intention of coming to look at anything," replied Prout, now becoming distinctly irritated, "because there is no need to do so. We shall continue precisely as planned, and I am pleased to say that Noreen has agreed that the Tableau of the Overthrow of Colonialism shall be the first item on the programme, as soon as the people arrive."

At this point, Southall gave up on Prout and went outside with Larsen.

"It's obviously hopeless trying to argue with him. Surely the best thing is simply to evacuate the station?"

"No, sir. There must be several hundred people here, and with all the other aircraft away you only have the Alouette. So you see, evacuation is not possible. The natives will be here too soon."

"Can't we radio for transport aircraft to Rabaul or Nouméa?"

"I'm sorry, sir, but it is out of the question. There is simply not enough time."

"Then what do you suggest?"

"I think, sir, your only hope is to persuade Fletcher to use his police," replied Larsen. "The man may be a brute, but at least he has a disciplined body of armed men under his command who are feared by the people."

"Yes, you're right, I'm afraid. I can't think he'll just stand by and allow them to wipe out his own kind. He's not an old colonial officer for nothing. We had better go up and see him.

Chapter XVI

A S SOON AS THE NEWS of the Morok advance had reached Ungabunga Fletcher had been woken by Moncreif with a jug of water in the face. His head reeling and his mouth tasting like the bottom of a baby's pram, he was slowly adjusting himself to the realities of the morning.

"I gather your delightful savages have run amok, and are advancing at this very moment with fire and sword on Ungabunga for a jolly morning's slaughter."

Fletcher slowly revolved his bloodshot eyes towards Moncreif and pondered these developments. Finally, he smiled.

"Well, looks like the orlies are goin' to get a bit more independence than Prout bargained on." He fumbled by the bed, and put his hand on a bottle of rum. After a long swig, he said, more brightly. "This should be better'n land dispute day!"

"From what I've seen of your chums, I don't think they'll be coming in a sporting mood. Genghis Khan on a bad day seems rather more likely, unless you do something to stop them."

"Stop them?" Fletcher suspended his contemplation of prolonged mayhem among his enemies with surprise and regret.

"You don't think they're going to care who's in their way once they really get going, do you?"

"Yeah, I s'pose yer right. I wouldn't want anything to happen to Angelina and Smithy. Yeah, yer right, dammit, I'll 'ave to stop 'em. Pity. I was lookin' forward to this."

Moncreif flung him a clean shirt and breeches, and while Fletcher dressed he went on:

"You realise if you can stop them, then you dictate terms to the Mission? You'll be master of the situation, the only force to protect them. And today the natives are supposed to ratify the new constitution."

"So?"

"Well, I'm no expert on Morok psychology, but if you handle them right, why not Fletcher for first President of Elephant Island?"

Fletcher grinned.

"Yer on, mate."

Shortly afterwards there was a loud banging on the front door. Larsen and Southall were rather surprised to find it opened promptly by an immaculate Fletcher.

"Yeah?" he greeted them coldly. "Bit early for a social call, in't it?"

Southall addressed him first, trying to be calm.

"Mr Fletcher, we've come to tell you that Morok war parties are coming to attack Ungabunga, and we must have your support. A lot of innocent lives are going to be lost unless you can stop them."

"Why don't yer send Prout? Let 'im bore 'em to death with one o' his lectures."

"I'm afraid Dr. Prout isn't quite himself this morning."

"Yeah, I'll bet! Sitting squirting in the dunny, most like."

Southall flinched, and desperately continued with his plea. "Well, he simply can't help us. We have absolutely no one to turn to but you. You can't let all the women and children be wiped out!"

"From the looks of that mob it'd be doin' 'em a favor—put 'em out of their misery."

"So," said Larsen, "Maybe you are perhaps afraid of the people?"

Fletcher looked at his hand, flexed his fingers, and pondered the attractions of a knuckle sandwich. Then he shrugged.

"Yeah, maybe I am, and maybe you've got tits. When I've had me breakfast, I'll get up there and sort 'em out." He shut the door in their faces.

Disconcerted by the coarseness of their reception, but feeling somewhat relieved, they started back to the Mission. In five minutes, Fletcher was at the barracks, rousting out the police, who shortly afterwards thundered out of Ungabunga in two squads divided between Fletcher, who took the track to Laripa, and the sergeant-major, who led his men towards Niovoro and Lavalava.

Soon afterwards the meeting in Hut 27 finally ground to its end. Prout sent them all off to their appointed tasks and decided to take a well-earned breather down on the strip. On the way he fell in with Moncreif, who was looking for Lord Southall.

"Well, Dr. Prout, it seems the Mission may have cause to be grateful to the abominable Fletcher after all."

"What can you mean?"

"Haven't you heard?"

"Heard *what*?"

"That Southall has asked him to take his police and persuade the Moroks to come to your party in a more amiable frame of mind."

"Are you telling me that Fletcher and his thugs are actually going to use force against the people, and with Lord Southall's approval?"

"Approval is putting it mildly, I'd say. Extreme keenness was my impression," said Moncreif. He walked off, laughing.

Prout was momentarily stunned by this utter betrayal of everything he had been working for, but suddenly he noticed the Alouette which had just been refuelled by Lt. Andreotti, Larsen's co-pilot. The lieutenant had seen the Special Commissioner at last night's banquet, and as Prout strode up he saluted.

"I am the Special Commissioner. Is this ready to fly?"

"Yes, sir."

"We have an emergency, a most serious crisis for the Mission. I need to be taken up the valley immediately. Can you do it?"

Young Andreotti was vastly flattered by this chance to be of service to the Special Commissioner himself, and readily offered to assist in any way he could. In a couple of minutes they were airborne, and before too long spotted Fletcher and his men approaching the great precipice of Oiburi-Naiburi. So, it was not too late. A little further on, the Morok war-party came into view, and Prout ordered Andreotti to set them down in a small clearing of level ground beside the track a hundred yards in front of the warriors. Despite his reverence for Prout, Andreotti was distinctly nervous.

"There's really nothing to worry about," said Prout. "I know the people, and they trust me. Put us down here."

He stepped out of the helicopter with absolute assurance and walked briskly towards the warriors, hailing them in the few words of the language he had managed to pick up.

"Peace, peace, my piglets! I laugh to see you in your polluted finery!"

The Moroks were stunned, less by his absurd attempts at flattery than by his sudden appearance among them. Abuk and Deng, allies for the day, were all in favor of dismembering the Father of Nyikang, deceiver and betrayer of all their hopes, there and then. Marbek took the longer view that they should carry him to Ungabunga and eat him ceremonially there as the high point of their festivities, but Garang strongly disagreed, on the grounds that red men's flesh was, from the religious point of view, an unknown quantity best left alone. He pointed out that the great precipice of Oiburi-Naiburi was just ahead, and suggested that throwing Prout over the edge would be highly acceptable to the spirit of the place, one Golumbuk, much feared as a mighty stirrer of landslides.

Convinced by Garang's reasoning, they made a sudden rush on Prout, overwhelmed him, and in a trice had him tied up and lashed to a pole. Andreotti, too far away to be of help, took off, but in his near-panic he misjudged his distance from the trees. One of the rotor blades clipped a tall pandanus-palm; the chopper turned over and plunged over the edge of the track down into the forest, crashing through the trees until it burst into flames a couple of hundred feet below. The Moroks watched it burn, entranced by the smoke and the explosions of the fuel tanks, and only then gave their full attention to Prout.

While all these events were unfolding in the mountains, Moncreif had sought out Lord Southall for an urgent private meeting in the Presidential Palace. As they sat on two gilded chairs in the Audience Chamber, Moncreif came briskly and brutally to the point.

"I don't suppose you can deny that Prout's policies have been a shambles. The question is what can be salvaged." Southall would have liked to object but could think of no cogent denial of the obvious, and so motioned for the lawyer to continue.

"Since the Mission is plainly incapable of continuing its administration here, our job is to find a way of extricating it and leaving at least a facade of political order behind. I have a proposal that should work."

"Yes?"

"Elections were to be held to choose an Assembly, and a President, but for obvious reasons we need to find our President today. We should choose Fletcher."

Southall was aghast.

"You can't be serious! He's a *white* man, quite apart from being a brute and an imperialist relic."

"In the first place, you don't have much choice since he's the only man who can save you. But looking at the long term, what better way of demonstrating the political maturity of a newly independent people, and their amazing ability to rise above old animosities, to say nothing of their dedication to inter-racial harmony and multiculturalism, than for them to choose a white man as their first President?"

Southall reflected.

"And of course," Moncreif continued, "you must take the credit for this remarkable triumph of political education, since it was your presence at a crucial time that proved decisive."

"But isn't there a Co-President to be elected in six months' time?"

"We shouldn't bother the people's heads with that sort of technicality," said Moncreif. "Since none of them can read, I rather doubt they'll hold it against us."

"Well, yes, I must agree that despite everything there's a great deal of force in what you say. In many ways it's a statesmanlike solution, but of course it all depends on whether Fletcher can stop them."

"I don't think we need worry too much on that score."

"A quadruple brandy, if you please, Angelina," said Oelrichs, in languid but penetrating tones. He was in the bar of the Cosmopolitan, as despite the panic in the Mission, he knew that Fletcher was quite capable of dealing with the Moroks and concluded that it was going to be a highly entertaining day. All the more reason, then, for enjoying his usual *apéritif* before luncheon.

"And perhaps you could let me have the menu?" Madame Negretti bustled over.

The Cosmopolitan was full of Mission personnel who had followed each other inside for company, rather in the spirit of sheep breaking into a field. The quadruple brandy had shocked them enough, and the spectacle of this repulsive sybarite actually reading a menu while a hideous death towered over them like a tidal wave was too much for Rebeccah Bloom.

"You'll be on the menu yourself, ya fat swine," she rasped, radiating malice.

"I think not, dear lady. The Moroks' taste in that direction inclines more to females, ah, well-*endowed* young females, if I may be so bold, though I won't distress you with the culinary details." He smiled cruelly, and Rebeccah fell silent.

"Now Angelina, I do hope the escargots are a little firmer of *flesh* than they were last week. And do I spy *kidneys?*"

"But Mr Oelrichs," quavered Daubeny, "you don't really think they'll eat us, do you?"

"Not immediately, I imagine. They usually like to indulge themselves in a spot of rape and torment their victims first. I'm afraid they haven't mastered the finer points of butchery, so they don't realise that for tenderness, the meat should be calm before it's slaughtered."

Miss Fratchett fixed a beady librarian's eye on Daubeny.

"I thought you told us that cannibalism was a myth?"

"I was just relying on Dr Prout," said the wretched boy. "Why isn't he here when we need him?"

There were general murmurs of agreement round the room, but at that moment Madame Negretti brought Oelrichs his escargots. As he sucked them noisily from their shells, the atmosphere in the room intensified to a frenzy, and from one corner came the unmistakable sound of vomiting.

"Are you just goin' to sit there stuffin' yer face and wait to be killed?" shrieked Noreen Hiscock, losing control.

"Ah, that is a contingency too remote to contemplate, madam. You see, I rather have the advantage of you all there, since I am

Oburabu, the sacred pig of the Moroks. Not terribly distinguished, but it should allow me to enjoy this afternoon's events in relative peace and comfort."

He paused to noisily devour the rest of the escargots. Wiping the butter from his chins, he continued.

"I was rather hoping for a chat with Dr. Prout myself before the end. So much to discuss, and so little time. Doesn't anyone know where he is?"

"Why should you want to speak to him?" said a voice from the back of the room. It was Phyllis, grey and stricken, who had hunted everywhere for her husband and had finally come to the hotel in the faint hope that someone might have seen him. "What could you possibly have to say to him? You sacred pig, indeed!"

"It's rather a matter of what he might have to say to us, isn't it? After all, it's quite an accomplishment—a whole United Nations Mission *horribly* exterminated in one afternoon. Even the great Southall has never managed that! Game, set, and match to your hubby, I should think."

"And what have you ever done to improve the world, you disgusting slug?"

"Nothing whatever, I'm pleased to say. If we all minded our own business, the world would revolve a good deal more steadily on its axis, and all of us would sleep more soundly in our beds, including you. Of course," he went on, "there *is* perhaps one way some of you might escape."

"How? Tell us! What do we do?"

"Well you know, it's native custom to appease a stronger force by offering them a few victims, and what they specially like is a few of the gentler sex—diverts their energies, don't y'know. It's up to you, of course, but if, say, Ms Bloom here, and your good self, Mrs. Prout, and perhaps Mrs. Hiscock were to display your ample charms before the advancing hordes it might at least slow them up. Allow them to slake their darker passions, you know."

"That's bloody disgustin'," burst out Cyril, who had been listening to this nightmarish monologue with horror and disbelief. "Givin' our womenfolk to a bunch of murderin' savages?"

"Well, of course, if it's against your principles, you can simply all be slaughtered together. Oh, excuse me, I think I see my kidneys coming."

All eyes turned to the kitchen door, where Moia, his best chef's hat slightly askew, entered with a steaming plate of devilled kidneys and placed them proudly in front of Oelrichs. As the fat man leant forward to inhale the aroma, and picked up his knife and fork, a wave of choking revulsion swept through the room and there was a general stampede for the door.

Prout had been tightly bound to a pole, in the manner of pigs and cannibal victims when carried to a feast. At first, in a torrent of garbled pidgin, he had tried to explain their mistake to them, until, tiring of his noise, they had stuffed a wad of leaves into his mouth. After struggling uselessly for a few minutes, he gave up and allowed them to bear him unresisting down the track.

As they walked along, it struck Garang that Prout had no idea why he had been so roughly handled, or what was going to happen to him, and, philosopher that he was, Garang considered that explaining this to Prout would add greatly to his agony. Looking around, his eye fell on young Padiang, whom he knew had some knowledge of Pidgin, and told him what he was to do. The young man came up alongside the Special Commissioner and, as they walked along, told him with relish why the people hated him and the Mission for betraying them by all their promises about the Houses of Filth, and despised them for their weakness, their cowardice, their folly, and their stupidity, and finally, gave him a concise but vivid summary of their general intentions that afternoon: the plunge over the great precipice that was intended for Prout, and the burning, the raping, the pillaging, and the general carnage that would follow at the Mission.

Prout was distraught and in tears, not only due to the horrors that awaited him and his fellow members of the Mission, but by the full extent of his own folly. Of course, his terrible mistake had been to allow the bestial Fletcher to remain on the island and turn the people against the Mission, instead of expelling him and his vile regime at the first opportunity, as he had been advised. The Moroks, too, he now realised with disgust, had deceived him, and under their amiable veneer, they were deeply reactionary and irrational peasants, utterly unworthy of the enlightened aid that he had sought to bring them, devious and ungrateful. They had let him down.

They soon reached Oiburi-Naiburi, and under the expert direction of Garang, who picked some leaves of the *tovapa* plant sacred to Golumbuk and tied them round the pole, they prepared to launch the Special Commissioner on his final journey. He, unfortunately, was rather too distracted in his last tormented moments of life to appreciate the beauty of the scene: the brilliant blue sky and the cool breeze that wafted over the edge of the precipice, rustling the grasses at the edge and bringing with it the distant roar of the Ungabunga river; the scent of some unknown flower all around them, and the cry of a bird-of-paradise from the forest above. The capture of the Special Commissioner and the fiery destruction of the helicopter were turning it into a lovely day for the Moroks, too, and they were so engrossed in preparing Prout for his departure that the sudden arrival of Fletcher and his men took them quite by surprise. Fletcher held up his hand in greeting.

"Men of Laripa, men of Dolivi, my friends. Ye have been betrayed by the Father of Nyikang, as I foretold. Did I not speak truth, eh?"

There were shouts of agreement.

"Aye," shouted Marbek, "But behold, O Tikame," and they brought forth the Special Commissioner, still trussed to his pole and ready for sacrifice. When he had recovered from his astonishment Fletcher said:

"I may be a bit dense, Prout, but what the hell kind of theory are you trying to prove now?"

Prout, gagged and writhing, could only stare malevolently.

"Father of Nyikang is my great enemy," Fletcher roared, "my persecutor, the burning hate of my heart, and he is mine to do with as I please. Know ye all this!" He fixed them for some moments with an inflexible gaze. Not a single voice was raised against him.

"As for his people of the Mission, they are but chickens under my protection, and ye shall not harm them. But ye shall have all that was promised you, their houses, their riches, their pressure lanterns, their scents, their shirts, their flash-lights, their motor-bikes, their brilliantine, their baby powder…!"

As the vista of wealth was unfolded before their limitless avarice the Moroks' thoughts of carnage gradually dissipated, and by the time Fletcher had exhausted his recitation of the red man's baubles, they were wholly converted to the new strategy. The sergeant-major had been told to use the same arguments with the Niovoro and Lavalava, and they found them equally persuasive.

Fletcher and the sergeant-major managed to keep up the Morok spirits, and by the time the two mobs reached Ungabunga, at about mid-day, they were actually in a jovial mood, some of them even breaking out from time to time in jolly pillaging songs. The police had gone ahead and were waiting, as on a land-dispute day, at the entrance to the station to quell the over-exuberant, and to allow Fletcher and the sergeant-major to catch up together with the main body.

Moncreif and Southall managed to quell the panic that Oelrichs had sparked among the Mission staff, and after packing them all off to the police barracks for safety, the two men had gone up to the top of the strip where they were waiting with the police in the shadow of the Gas Works when the Moroks arrived.

Fletcher, standing before them, raised his hand for silence, and addressed his children.

"The words of Tikame are true. The words of Tikame never fail. What he has promised you, this day he will deliver into your hands. Go, now, into all the houses of your enemies, and seize what you desire!" With a mighty wave of his arm he gave the Mission over to be sacked and, like a dam bursting, the flood of screaming Moroks poured down the strip and engulfed the homes and warehouses. When Fletcher saw that they were happily occupied, he rode over to Moncreif and Southall with Prout being carried along behind him by the police.

Southall was extremely agitated.

"I thought you were going to save the Mission, Fletcher. What have you done?"

"Saved your bloody lives, mate, that's what. The deal is they take all the goodies they like and they lay off your people. O'course, they could've taken the goodies and put you in the stew pot as well, but they were willing enough to take what was on offer."

"Yes, yes," said Southall. "I quite see that. It's the best that could have been done. In fact, in the circumstances, I must congratulate you. Now Moncreif and I have been discussing this question of independence…" and they went on to explain their plans for Fletcher's elevation to the Presidency of Elephant Island without delay.

There was a strangled cry of rage from the trussed bundle on its pole, and Fletcher smiled coldly.

"Hadn't we better ask Dr. Prout about that?" he said, and he pointed to the Special Commissioner.

"Good God, what on earth has happened to him?" said Southall, who hadn't recognized the unfortunate figure suspended from the pole. Fletcher gave them a brief explanation of how he had saved Prout's life, and how the Special Commissioner had got himself into that predicament in the first place.

Southall looked down at Prout. "I'm afraid you've become a serious embarrassment to the United Nations, Sydney. I would suggest an extended period of leave with immediate effect," and he turned back to Fletcher and Moncreif.

"I am now the senior United Nations representative, so there's no legal difficulty about it. I understand it would be best if we held a short ceremony, in which I proclaim you as the new President, and Moncreif here swears you in. I should mention that I have persuaded him to accept the office of Chief Justice."

Moncreif bowed to Fletcher with a sardonic smile. The President-designate laughed.

"Perhaps," Southall went on, "you could arrange the details of the ceremony?"

"Right. No worries. I'll get the police to organize it. Like land-dispute day—they know the drill." He strode off to give his orders.

After an hour or so of strenuous plundering, sated with pillage and staggering under the bizarre accumulations of their chosen loot, even the Moroks needed a rest to regain their strength for further pursuits such as arson and general demolition, and it was during this lull that they heard the familiar notes of the bugle from the top of the strip. There was a general drift in that direction, and there they found Fletcher flanked by most of the police, with Lord

Southall, Moncreif and Oelrichs, Smith and Madame Negretti and, oddly enough, Tristram Daubeny. In front of them was a ceremonial dais decorated with some pots of lupins hastily borrowed from Madame Negretti.

It was a warm afternoon, with bright sunshine, and the Moroks were happy to sit on the grass, picking over their booty with dirty, inquisitive fingers, waiting to see what would happen next. Fletcher, Southall, and Moncreif mounted the dais and Southall began his speech to a newly independent nation. Unfortunately, he only spoke English, so Daubeny had been hastily recruited to translate into Pidgin, with one of the Morok interpreters to translate from Pidgin into the language of the people. Southall addressed them in the words of a seasoned statesman.

"My dear friends, it warms my heart to be with you here today, a special day we have all been waiting for, and to have the honour of celebrating your new Independence with you. The United Nations administration has always planned to allow you to achieve your freedom from colonial rule as soon as possible, with the government of your choice. So I believe we shall discharge our mandate most fully for you if I propose your trusted leader, Mr. Roger Fletcher, as your new President, to light your path into the future. Please join wholeheartedly with me in acclaiming him."

The speech, as the Moroks heard it in their own language, went as follows:

"My lustful little things. It inflames my bowels to be with you at this pig-killing, which is very late, and to stuff your mouths with giblets as we all enjoy ourselves. We have been plotting for a long time to let you cast aside all restraint with wild abandon and do whatever you like. So today we shall vomit all over you to celebrate Tikame as your new chief, who will lead you in burning down things for ever and ever. Please bugger me hard and sing songs about him."

This amazing piece of eloquence was at first greeted by stunned silence, and then by a growing wave of laughter mixed with cheers, which soon gave way to a cheerful Morok anthem about the joys of rapine, arson, and premeditated homicide.

"Do you think I hit the right note?" asked Southall, rather apprehensively. The new President, who was feeling in a generous mood, clapped him on the back with a grin and said:

"Don't worry, mate. I reckon that's the best damned speech yer'll ever make."

When the festivities were over, President Fletcher set about installing a Ministry of All the Talents, including Garang as Archbishop of Ungabunga, Marbek as Minister of War and General Destruction, Abuk as Minister of Feasts, Smith in charge at the Ministry of Recuperation, Moncreif promoted to Lord Chancellor, and Erny as Entertainment Secretary, and everything slowly got back more or less to normal.

Prout, betrayed by the people he had come to help, and humiliated by the United Nations whom he had served so faithfully, immediately sent in his resignation, which was accepted with relief, but he was soon invited by the European Commission to bring his unique talents to Brussels. What he called "the only truly rational administration in the world" proved to be his natural home, and while he has remained largely unknown to the general public, some of the directives from the Commission over the years have revealed the unmistakable hand of the master.

When last heard of, he was reputed to be working on the Metric Year.

CPSIA information can be obtained
at www.ICGtesting.com
Printed in the USA
BVOW06s0853100317
478068BV00008B/163/P